Changing Shifts

Swapping lives, finding love!

In London, widowed pediatrician Georgie is struggling with everyone's sympathy when no one knows her husband was having an affair.

In Edinburgh, pediatrician Clara's dreams of having a family lie in tatters as her ex parades his new love around.

Through a job-swap website, Georgie and Clara impulsively swap cities and hospitals to escape their real lives and embark on new adventures!

But when they arrive at their new destinations, both women find the last thing either wants or expects—romance!

Read Georgie's story in
Fling with Her Hot-Shot Consultant

And Clara's story in
Family for the Children's Doc

Both available now!

Dear Reader,

Sometimes writing a book is just fun. The Changing Shifts duo came about after a brainstorming session with fellow author Kate Hardy, who wanted us to have two entirely different characters who swapped places for a while.

As we both write medical romances, each book had to have a realistic medical setting, along with a life swap brought about when both characters need it. Different landscapes. Family dynamics. Adjusting to new people and new places, with a brother and sister to help connect the stories.

Joshua Woodhouse has trust issues, but he can't really see that until he finds a woman who makes him curious about life again. Clara Connolly is a medic with a long history of depression. She works hard to manage her condition and not let it impact her professional life. Both of these characters were crying out to me to tell their stories and give them their happy-ever-after.

I've worked with many health-care professionals who live with mental health issues. It's widely known, but rarely spoken about, and I wanted to include it in a story with the care it deserves. I hope you agree.

Best wishes,

Scarlet Wilson

FAMILY FOR THE CHILDREN'S DOC

SCARLET WILSON

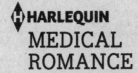

MEDICAL
ROMANCE

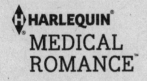

ISBN-13: 978-1-335-14950-3

Family for the Children's Doc

This edition published by arrangement with Harlequin Books S.A.

For questions and comments about the quality of this book,
please contact us at CustomerService@Harlequin.com.

Harlequin Enterprises ULC
22 Adelaide St. West, 40th Floor
Toronto, Ontario M5H 4E3, Canada
www.Harlequin.com

Printed in U.S.A.

Scarlet Wilson wrote her first story at age eight and has never stopped. She's worked in the health service for twenty years, having trained as a nurse and a health visitor. Scarlet now works in public health and lives on the West Coast of Scotland with her fiancé and their two sons. Writing medical romances and contemporary romances is a dream come true for her.

Books by Scarlet Wilson

Harlequin Medical Romance

London Hospital Midwives

Cinderella and the Surgeon

The Good Luck Hospital

Healing the Single Dad's Heart
Just Friends to Just Married?

Locked Down with the Army Doc
Island Doctor to Royal Bride?
Tempted by the Hot Highland Doc

Harlequin Romance

The Cattaneos' Christmas Miracles

Cinderella's New York Christmas

The Italian Billionaire's New Year Bride

Visit the Author Profile page
at Harlequin.com for more titles.

This book has to be dedicated to my fellow author and partner in crime, Kate Hardy. Thanks for the fun of doing a duo together and making it such fun.

PROLOGUE

CLARA CONNOLLY SMILED and tried to keep the awkward expression plastered on her face as she watched her ex, Harry, affectionately put his arm around the waist of Gerta, his latest girlfriend, and brush a kiss at the side of her temple as they walked into one of the lifts together.

She could sense a few sets of curious eyes turn towards her in the busy main foyer of St Christopher's Hospital in Edinburgh; hence the plastered smile on her face. She wasn't quite sure what message she was trying to send. Indifference? Happiness? The truth was either would do. She'd only dated Harry for a few months—and he certainly hadn't been the love of her life. He'd been more like a pleasant passing phase. In a way she was glad he'd met someone who made his heart leap up and down. And even gladder that he'd managed to tell her, before the rest of the world found out.

That was the trouble with dating someone from work. The constant possibility of running into each other when the relationship ended. And while she was happy enough for Harry and Gerta, it reminded her that the ticking of her biological clock had started to amplify in her head. She pressed her lips together, letting the smile slip from her face as she waited for the next lift to arrive and take her up to the paediatric ward. It was weird. She was only thirty. But just about everyone she knew had met their 'happy ever after' by now. Clara just seemed to flit from one unfulfilling relationship to another. No big drama. No heartache. Just a general feeling of…emptiness.

It wasn't as if there was no one in her life. She had her best friend Ryan—who was just as unlucky in love as she was. She had a good group of friends, most of whom were now married, pregnant or with at least one child. It amplified her feelings. She had her own place—a cottage in a village on the outskirts of Edinburgh, surrounded by gorgeous farmland and countryside. It was usually her saving grace after a busy shift, but in the last few weeks she'd become more conscious of the space around her, and how quiet her life had become. Last night, after a single glass of wine, she'd found herself looking into sperm donation and seriously considering it. She'd always wanted to be a mother. Sure, she might have thought she would find someone to share the joy of parenthood with, but the more she looked, the less she found any real candidates.

Why not? She was a successful woman with her own place and a good job. There was no reason she couldn't bring up a child on her own. The question was—did she really want to?

Family was important to her—and she had a good one. Her mum and dad had retired to Spain a few years ago and had a better social life than she did. Her brother, Euan, was an engineer in Australia, married with three kids under five. She'd honestly never seen him look happier. Every time she video chatted with either her parents or her brother, there was always that little question—*Have you met anyone yet?*—and she understood; her family just wanted her to be settled and happy, because they knew she wanted that too. But the question was starting to ruffle her normally good nature. It wasn't as if she could just magic Mr Perfect out of nowhere.

She knew that her mother had always wanted a large, chaotic family. But pre-eclampsia had put paid to that idea, with Clara being told that both she and her mother were lucky to be alive. It had weighed on her mind throughout her life. With her brother being so far away, it felt as if the pressure was on to provide grandchildren her parents could see frequently. And the truth was, she might have had similar hopes to her mother—a life filled with children was always what entered her brain when she dreamed about the future.

The doors to the lift slid open and a few minutes later she was on her own ward. She could see the city landscape through the windows. The familiar sights of the edge of the castle in the distance and the Scott Monument usually made her feel grounded, but today they just left an uncomfortable feeling in her stomach. She quickly checked over the patients, reviewing the diagnoses for those who had been admitted overnight, and rechecking the children who'd already been on her ward. She had just finished talking to some parents about their baby son, who'd been admitted with a chest infection, when her colleague, Bea, came into the office with coffee in both hands.

She slid one over the desk to Clara. 'You've still got that look on your face.'

'What look?' Clara glanced up from the screen where she was ordering tests.

'That look that seems to say *I'm trying to*

pretend to the world I'm fine when I'm really not.'

Clara took one sip of the coffee then wrinkled her brow. 'What do you mean?'

She'd worked with Bea, one of the senior nurses here, for the last five years. They were friends. Bea wasn't known for playing her cards close to her chest. Clara liked straight talkers. It was probably why they got on so well together.

Bea sighed. 'Ever since we had that kid—Ben Shaw—you've had a look about you. One that makes it seem like you come here because you *have* to—not because you want to. You never looked like that before. Something has to give, Clara. And I'm just worried it's going to be you.'

Clara swallowed back the immediate lump in her throat. Ben Shaw had been admitted overnight a few months ago. Clara had been out sick with norovirus. Any occurrence for a member of staff meant an automatic ban of forty-eight hours from being in contact with patients, and a locum doctor had covered the shift. Ben had been admitted with abdominal pain, for review in the morning.

But as soon as Clara had stepped onto the ward she'd known immediately what was wrong with the toddler. Bowel obstruction was uncommon in kids—and hard to spot for someone inexperienced.

Ben had been rushed to surgery, but had ultimately lost part of his bowel. The delay in diagnosis had been life-changing, and Clara just couldn't shake that *what if* feeling.

Bea reached over and squeezed her hand as Clara stared at the screen in front of her, watching it grow a bit blurry. All the stuff about Ben had affected her, left her feeling a bit numb. Flat, even.

It had happened more than once to her before. She'd first been diagnosed with depression as a teenager and it had remained in her life ever since. Sometimes she was good. Sometimes she was bad. Sometimes she needed someone to talk to, and medication to make her feel a bit better. Most people who knew her had no idea. Clara had always played her cards close to her chest, especially about her mental health. It didn't matter that one in three of all doctors were supposedly affected by mental health issues at some point in their life, it was still something that wasn't really discussed. When she'd had to take a few months off from medical school her family and tutors had been extremely supportive; she'd even got to delay an important exam and take it at a later date. But she still didn't like to tell anyone about it.

She bit her lip and sat back, reaching for the coffee with both hands. 'It's just been a hard few months. What with Ben, then the break-up with Harry, and stuff going on with Ryan.'

'What's going on with Ryan?' asked Bea.

Clara ran her hands through her hair. 'Can you keep a secret?'

Bea nodded. Ryan McGregor was a fellow doctor in the hospital and Clara's best friend and she knew he liked to keep things low-key about his disastrous love life.

'He's having a really hard time. He's going through a difficult divorce and just can't seem to get out of the hole he's dug himself into. He's having to come and stay at mine for a few days until he gets things sorted.'

Bea frowned and Clara added, 'They've sold the house and he's having trouble find-ing someone who will rent to him until he can find something he wants to buy.'

Bea gave a brief nod. 'Because of his dog?' She took a sip of coffee as Clara nodded in return. 'He adores that dog, doesn't he? But lots of places up for rent around the city won't allow pets. He might be at yours longer than you think.'

Clara blinked back the tears that had

brimmed in her eyes. 'I just don't know what to do to help him.'

They exchanged glances and Clara could tell Bea knew she wasn't talking about the housing situation or the dog.

Bea gave a thoughtful nod and leaned forward. 'It's hard to support your friends emotionally, when you don't feel safe in that place yourself.'

It was as if someone had just thrown a blanket over her and given her a giant hug. The guilt that had been playing on her mind over these last few weeks finally had a little outlet. She could hardly push her pathetic worries onto Ryan, not when he had so much to worry about himself—it would be selfish of her to try and talk about it. But that glance from Bea felt like enough. Even saying the words out loud felt like a slight easing of the dark cloud that had settled around her.

Her mood had been low recently and she hadn't really wanted to admit it to anyone. But last week she'd done a postnatal depression questionnaire with a young mum she'd been worried about, and some of the answers to the questions had made her stop and think about how *she* would answer them. Not that she had a baby, or anything. But just that simple act had made her suck in a breath and take a long, hard look at herself.

'I should be fine,' she said determinedly. 'I should be getting on with things and pulling my life together. I'm not dependent on anyone. I have a good job, my own place. I should be happy.'

'But you're not,' said Bea matter-of-factly. 'Who are you trying to convince—me, or you?'

Clara heaved in a deep breath. 'No,' she admitted, 'I'm not.'

They sat in silence for a few seconds while Clara thought about what she'd just said out loud. It hadn't been quite as scary as she'd thought. Maybe it was Bea—maybe it was her intuition and understanding, mixed in with her ability to get straight to the point. Bea didn't know that Clara had actually taken the step of visiting her own GP a few days ago. Her hand went to her pocket and fastened around the packet of tablets she had in there. She hadn't decided yet whether to take them or not. She recognised that she probably needed them. When life started to seem a bit black around the edges she knew she had to do something. She couldn't quite believe how much the young mum's face had mirrored her own. This conversation was giving her a bit of clarity, a sign. The reassurance that she needed. Her fingers tightened around the meds a little more. She could do this. Depression wasn't a sign of weakness. Lots of her friends and colleagues in similarly stressful jobs had suffered throughout the years. Recognising it, seeing her GP and accepting the prescription were only the first steps. It was time to take the next one. Clara gave a half-smile and gave Bea a grateful look. 'I love working with you. You don't let me get away with anything.'

Bea licked her lips and gave a gentle shake of her head. 'This conversation isn't over. I'm not going to let you leave it here. We're friends—it's my job to tell you that you need to give yourself a bit of space to decide what you really want in life, Clara. You're young, you're a beautiful girl. You're a great doctor. But is that enough? Maybe you just need a change of scenery. A chance to get away from things.' She held up her hands. 'Sometimes we get in a rut. Sometimes we need to try something new.' She pointed to a flyer on the noticeboard to the side of Clara. 'Why don't you think about that?'

Clara wrinkled her nose and turned to look at the slightly crumpled flyer that had been on the board for a few months. She'd seen it but never really given it much thought. It was advertising the opportunity to do a job swap elsewhere in the UK for six months.

She laughed. 'What are the chances of another paediatric registrar wanting to job swap for six months? And the chances of the job being in a place I might actually want to go?'

Bea stood up and lifted the cups, raising her eyebrows. There was a slight glint in her eye. 'Well, you won't know if you don't try,' she replied in her mischievous manner, before giving Clara a wink and heading out of the door.

For a few minutes Clara just sat there. She'd actually vocalised how she was feeling, and everything Bea had shot back at her had been true. She wasn't feeling great, and she couldn't put her finger on exactly why. There wasn't one big thing, just a whole host of little things that were bubbling under the surface and giving her a general sense of unhappiness and discontent. She hated that. It made her feel not like *herself*.

But she didn't really feel entitled to be unhappy. Most of her friends would give her a list of reasons why she should be delighted with her life, and in most cases they would be right.

But the fact was, she couldn't help how she

was feeling. She slipped the first tablet out of its packaging and swallowed it. There. Baby steps. But maybe she should try something else too?

She bit her lip as she put in all the orders for the tests required for the patients on the ward. Then she opened another window on the computer and automatically typed in the website address from the flyer. She didn't even have to look up at the poster—it seemed to have imprinted on her brain.

It only took a minute to put in her details: name, job, home address and a few clinical details. She uploaded a few photos of her house she had on her phone. She'd taken them just the other day to send to her brother in Australia. The next box was the hard part. Where was she looking for a job? She shook her head and just left it open. Fate. She'd leave it to fate.

The spinning egg timer of doom appeared on the screen in front of her. She groaned. Chances were the website had just died, or the search was too wide and the system couldn't cope. Any time the whirling egg timer appeared on a computer screen in front of her, it generally meant bad news.

She pushed her chair back, ready to go back

out onto the ward, as the screen blinked and then changed.

Her mouth fell open. There was a match. One.

She leaned forward and read everything on the screen. London. In the Royal Hampstead Free Hospital. *No way.* That place had just as good a reputation as St Christopher's. Why would anyone want to job swap from there?

Her heart gave a flutter. Fate. She'd left it to fate. And fate had answered. One job opportunity in a place with a fabulous reputation. Pictures of a flat that looked very swanky. This was just too good to be true.

There was a big button on the screen, inviting her to find out more. For the first time in a long time her heart gave a little leap.

She hesitated for only the briefest of seconds before reaching out and clicking on it.

London. Get ready for Clara Connolly.

CHAPTER ONE

Two weeks later

SHE WAS CRAZY. She was definitely crazy. Yesterday she'd been finishing her last day working in Edinburgh, going back to her cute cottage with a view of the Scottish countryside and being disturbed by one of the sheep pressing its face up against her kitchen window. All entirely normal.

Now, she was circling the same confusing streets of London over and over again, sweat trickling down her back as she realised there was absolutely nowhere to park.

She hadn't thought to ask about parking. It hadn't even crossed her mind. She'd assumed that there would be somewhere convenient and close to the flat to leave her car... and was learning quickly just how wrong that assumption was.

Some of the streets had no parking at all.

Others only had parking for permit holders. One car park charged thirty pounds a day. Thirty pounds? She wanted to laugh out loud.

The drive down from Edinburgh had started well. She'd left plenty of time in case of delays—and there had been many. A collision on the motorway near Newcastle had slowed traffic, followed by horrendous roadworks near Doncaster. By the time she'd hit London her timing had been way off, and it was clear she was in the rush hour. It didn't help that her satnav seemed to have forgotten a vital update and had a completely different idea of which streets were one-way and which streets were totally blocked off. By the time the tenth black cab driver tooted at her, shaking his head, she was close to tears.

Clara had always prided herself on her driving skills. Touch wood, she'd never been in an accident or even had a near miss before. One hour in London and she'd almost had one head-on collision and more near misses than she wanted to admit. By the time she finally saw the sleek tower block near Canary Wharf that had the correct address, her nerves were more than a little frayed.

She pulled up outside the building, ignoring all the signs that told her not to stop, and

got out, slamming her door and sucking in a
breath of the warm, clammy air.

A man leaving the smart building frowned
as she strode past him, trying to see if there
was anyone who could give her some direc-
tions about where to park. Her car was stuffed
full of her possessions. Surely she was allowed
to unload?

The front wall of the foyer was completely
glass, with the building at a slight angle, facing towards Canary Wharf. There was a bank
of small boxes to her left and she scanned
them, finding 14C and keying in the appropriate code. She sighed in relief at the sight of
the silver key, a cream key fob and the slim
electronic card—apparently both the key and
the card opened the door to the flat.

She glanced back at her car, wondering if
she should go back and grab some things before heading up in the lift, but curiosity got
the better of her. She wanted to see her home
for the next six months.

The silver doors glided open and she barely
felt the lift move before they opened again on
the fourteenth floor. A short walk down the
corridor took her to the flat and she scanned
the card in front of the round pad, letting the
door click open.

As she pushed inside her breath caught

somewhere in her throat. The sun had lowered in the sky and the whole apartment was bathed in warm light.

Everything was so clean-looking! The entrance hall had smooth cream tiles, leading to a matching immaculate kitchen on her right that opened out to a largish sitting room furnished with three curved cream sofas, a glass table and TV set into the left side wall. But it was the view that was the most spectacular. Windows took up the entire facing wall, showing all the beauty of Canary Wharf, just a stone's throw away. Her feet moved automatically, carrying her over to the windows, and she realised quickly they weren't windows but, in fact, concertina-style doors. She fumbled for the button then pushed them open, stepping out onto the balcony beyond.

It wasn't quite on the edge of the dock, but it was close enough that she could see the activity on the dockside. There was a row of restaurants and bars, boats bobbing on the water. The busy noise of people finishing their day at work and hitting the bars and restaurants below floated across the air beneath her, along with the aromas of food, making her stomach growl.

She looked out across the London skyline, spotting the event arena and the snaking river beyond. She really was here. She'd done this. She'd left Scotland behind and made a change. For a few seconds she closed her eyes, leaning against the balcony barrier and breathing in the warm air again, letting the different sensations surround her. It was certainly warmer than it was back home, but her skin prickled.

She opened her eyes again and almost jolted at the view again. Several of the tower blocks around the dock were dotted with lights, sending a purple and pink glow shimmering back upwards from the water. It was beautiful, but could take a bit of getting used to. She spun back around, putting her hands behind her and looking back inside the flat.

This place wasn't like any flat she'd been in before. It was like a show home, decked out in gorgeous pieces of furniture, all ergonomically placed. If it wasn't for the few scattered cushions and the row of books in a nearby bookcase, she might believe no one even lived here.

Her stomach curled as she thought of her inelegant squishy sofa back home, dark stone walls and temperamental fire. She prayed that Ryan had tidied up the way he'd promised and left the welcoming note and food before he left.

Clara left the doors open and wandered

through the rest of the flat. The bedroom was just as immaculate as everywhere else, with white bedlinen and a big comfortable pink throw at the end of the bed. A space had been cleared for her in the closet and Clara resisted the temptation of looking to see what clothes her counterpart had left behind.

There was a nice writing desk looking out at the view across London, with a bottle of champagne sitting on it, tied with a big pink ribbon and note.

I thought if you were anything like me you'd need some of this after your long journey.

There's a secret chocolate stash in the drawer on the right and I did an online order for food that, hopefully, Louie the concierge has left in the kitchen for you.

Any problems, give him a dial on 01 and he'll be happy to help.

Other than that, enjoy London!

Georgie xx

Clara couldn't resist; she slid open the drawer on the right to see a whole array of chocolate. Dark chocolate mints, milk chocolate orange, foil-wrapped caramels and a huge sea salted caramel bar.

Things were definitely looking up.

She frowned. Concierge? She hadn't noticed anyone behind the desk in the foyer. She walked back to the kitchen and opened the gleaming fridge. Sure enough, milk, butter, eggs, cheese and bacon were waiting for her, along with a variety of fruit and vegetables in the cool drawer. In one of the cupboards she found bread, some pasta and a few jars, enough to make dinner for a few nights. Her stomach growled loudly. It was so nice. So considerate. But what she really wanted right now was pizza.

Clara sighed and made her way back downstairs to gather the rest of her possessions. It would probably take her at least an hour to lug everything back up and get unpacked.

The foyer was still empty and a traffic warden was frowning outside. She ran out, muttering excuses and opening her car door before he had a chance to start scribbling. He raised one eyebrow and pointed to a slim, almost hidden downward ramp directly on the right of the building. 'Emergency vehicles only out here,' he muttered. 'Why don't you use the parking underneath?'

Underground parking. Of course a place like this would have parking for residents. But the angle of the building meant she hadn't been able to glimpse it from the road. She gave a flustered nod and climbed back in, starting her car and swinging it in an uneven arc as she tried to line up her large four-by-four with the narrow lane.

Clara sucked in a breath as she edged her car down the narrow ramp. She knew it was ridiculous—as if she could actually make her ungainly four-by-four smaller! For the first time in her life she regretted being behind the wheel of the wide, sturdy vehicle. It was perfect for farm roads in Scotland, but not exactly ideal for slim underground parking entrances.

It was dark—much darker than seemed normal. Weren't there lights down here? Shouldn't they at least come on when a car entered? This was like something from a horror movie. Any minute now the weird axe man would jump onto the bonnet of her car.

She flicked on her car lights and came to an abrupt halt at the low-slung gleaming red car in front of her. Her breath caught in her throat. Darn it—that was close. What was it about London and driving for her?

She turned her head from side to side, trying to scan the underground parking area. It didn't seem the biggest in the world, and with no other lighting it was going to be hard to manoeuvre her large car. It was too old to have parking sensors, and she didn't even want to think about what kind of luxury vehicles could be hidden down here.

She edged forward, seeing some white lines, and tried to swing into a space. Her headlights lit up the side of another car and she let out an expletive as she moved forward and back, trying to get into the space. It was like being a learner all over again.

These weren't the biggest spaces in the world, she couldn't see properly and she was tired after her long journey. All she really wanted to do was grab her stuff, get back upstairs and open that bottle of champagne.

She finally stopped edging forward and back and shimmied out of her car, taking care not to touch the neighbouring car with her door. Sweat was running down her back. The capital was much warmer than back home. She hadn't really thought about that when she'd planned her wardrobe.

In the dark, she fumbled around the car and opened the boot, grabbing at her boxes in the low light within. She was only taking the boxes that carried the bare essentials—she had no intention of coming back down here tonight. Clara wasn't easily intimidated but being alone in a strange dark car park would unnerve anyone. She stuck one box on top of the roof of her car as she grabbed another three. In the far corner of the dark parking space she could see a small blue square glowing—that had to be the lift. At least she'd be able to get back upstairs. Hopefully, tomorrow she'd get a chance to talk to the concierge about the lighting down here. Or at least find somewhere to buy a flashlight.

As if by magic, the lights came on all around her as she reached up to close the boot. She jerked. The box at the top of her pile teetered then spilled onto the concrete floor.

Clara groaned as another car glided down the ramp. The driver paused, scowling at her, before sweeping into a space opposite. Friendly type then.

She dropped to her knees, stuffing toiletries and underwear back into the box as fast as she could. Last thing she wanted was Mr Grumpy getting an uninvited view of her smalls.

There were a few muffled sounds next to her. She looked up. The guy was carrying a sleeping bundle in his arms, the scowl still firmly in place as he swept past her.

'At least try and park in your own space,' he muttered as his long strides ate up the ground under his feet.

She blinked from her position on the ground. Now the lights were on, she could see that each parking space had a number. The parking space she was in was labelled 24F. Oops.

She glanced down the long slim space, trying to work out the numbering. If she'd got this right, 14C would be right down at the other end. Great. Further to carry her boxes. Should she move her car? Maybe not right now. Now there were some lights she could do it when she came back down to collect the rest of her things. She jumped up quickly and hurried after the man.

He was tall, over six feet, with broad shoulders and an irritatingly quick stride. The doors to the lift slid open and he stepped inside.

'I'm sorry,' she said quickly, still walking towards the lift. 'I couldn't see what I was doing. The lights didn't come on when I came down and I haven't had a chance to speak to the concierge yet and—'

She was babbling. She knew she was babbling.

He spun around and she sucked in a breath. Darn it, he was handsome. *Really* handsome. Dark hair, tall, muscular structure, a shadow around his jaw line and penetrating eyes. And it struck her that it had been a while since she'd noticed something like that.

For the last few months all men had just merged into one. This was the first time she'd actually *noticed* someone in a long time. Her brain gave a hopeful flicker of recognition. Too bad it seemed that he was as arrogant as he was handsome.

It didn't help that she was still babbling— and she hated appearing nervous. Especially in front of a man whose sole intention seemed to be to frown at her and look at her as if she was something on the bottom of his shoe. How dare he? Wasn't he even going to try and be slightly friendly?

This was a horrible situation. He clearly lived here—last thing she wanted was to make an enemy of someone who'd be her neighbour for the next six months. But, on the other hand, he could clearly see that she'd just arrived. Couldn't he give her a break?

No. Those dark blue eyes were still glaring at her. There was a noise behind her—a sliding sound, followed by an ear-splitting car alarm that made them both jump. The child in his arms gave a start and instantly started crying.

She turned around to see the box she'd left balanced on the roof of her car had now vanished, and the car next to hers was the one with the screeching alarm. The words formed on her lips, 'Oh, sorry...' and she turned back just in time to see the lift doors slide closed and the man turn his back on her.

Clara heaved in an enormous sigh. 'Welcome to London, Clara,' she muttered as the lights flickered out around her and plunged her into darkness. Again.

CHAPTER TWO

JOSHUA WOODHOUSE WAS not having a good day.

Correct that. He wasn't having a good week. Not since his sister had sprung the fact on him that she was transferring her post for six months and disappearing to Scotland at short notice. He still couldn't get over it. Had Georgie been unhappy? Depressed? Bored? Why hadn't he realised? She'd denied all those things, just telling him she needed a change of scene for a while. The truth was, he couldn't blame her. Her husband had been killed in an accident a while ago, and Georgie just seemed to have carried on. In fact, she'd continued working in his paediatric department in the Royal Hampstead Free, *and* continued to help him out with his young daughter, Hannah.

He'd kept pressing. And so Georgie had told him the real reason she was leaving and he'd wanted to slap himself. Her husband had been having an affair. Joshua had been shocked.

He'd had absolutely no idea, and neither, apparently, had Georgie, finding out only after her husband had died. At first, he'd felt a flare of anger that she'd kept secrets from him. But she'd quickly put him in his place, letting him know that it was her business, and up to her to decide if she wanted to share. Guilt had swamped him. He should have been a better support to his sister, instead of just thanking her for continuing to show up at work and helping out at a moment's notice with Hannah. He should have realised something else was going on. But he hadn't stopped to ask. And now his sister had decided she needed a change of scene for six months.

What could he say when he'd apparently already let her down so badly? Of course, he had to see her off to Scotland with his complete blessing, no matter how he felt about it.

He had too many balls in the air at once. He knew that. Being Head of Department at one of the busiest hospitals in London, as well as being sole carer for his young daughter, sometimes made him feel as if he couldn't think straight.

There had been a nanny. But two days after Georgie had told him about her job swap, he'd got a tearful call from her to say her father had been diagnosed with terminal cancer back in Sweden. It had struck a chord, and he'd booked her a flight home with his blessing, and the knowledge that she wouldn't be returning. It had added yet another ball to juggle and he'd had to hire someone at short notice who he hoped would work out for himself and Hannah.

His parents kept telling him to move closer to them in Norfolk—they loved their granddaughter and would gladly help out. As it was, they came to London frequently to help when they could. But part of him didn't want to push his responsibility onto them.

Hannah was *his* daughter. He had to be the constant in her life. Her mother had died three weeks after delivering their new baby, having been diagnosed with acute myeloid leukaemia. It had taken him a while to come to terms with the fact that Abby had realised she was sick while she was in the late stages of pregnancy, and waited until she'd delivered before telling anyone. Hindsight was a horrible thing. The tiredness. The paleness. The few bruises.

He'd spent the first few months blaming himself while caring for a brand-new baby. But time had given him perspective. Anyone who'd known Abby would have known that she'd never have put her life before her child's. They'd lost a pregnancy the year before, and so she'd been determined to do everything possible to make sure their little girl arrived safely. Her determination was one of the many reasons that he'd loved her.

Her leukaemia had been so aggressive that her chance of survival had been virtually nil. Conversations with colleagues had helped him understand that no matter when she'd admitted to knowing about her illness, the outcome would have inevitably been the same. And the sad fact was, they would have doubtless spent the last few weeks of her pregnancy arguing, with him pushing her to deliver early and seek treatment—of any kind—in an attempt to stretch out their time together.

Instead, they'd spent the time looking forward to the birth of their daughter, with only a few anxious weeks after she'd arrived to consider the future. The ending had been inevitable but peaceful, and whilst Joshua had been angry at the fragility of life, he'd had the opportunity to tell his wife how much he loved her and listen to all her hopes and dreams for Hannah in the future. Abby had even written a diary for their daughter, a list of instructions for him, and some letters to give to Hannah in the future. Whilst lucky wasn't a word he would choose to describe their situation, he'd been a doctor long enough to know that many families didn't get a final opportunity to talk and plan and he should count his blessings that they had.

Hannah was the image of her mother with the same pale blue eyes and fine brown hair. Even though she'd barely met Abby, she had some of the same habits and tendencies. If Josh didn't witness it on a daily basis he wouldn't have believed it, and it had changed his thinking countless times on the nature or nurture debate.

His phone buzzed and he pulled it from his pocket. Georgie, letting him know that things had been 'interesting' when she'd arrived last night and that she was looking forward to her first day.

Something flickered in his brain and he groaned as he walked out onto the ward. He'd been so rushed last night—picking up Hannah from after school care and taking her straight to ballet lessons. No wonder she'd fallen asleep in the car on the way home. But now he had a horrible inkling about the strange woman in the garage last night. And, as if life was trying to teach him a lesson, standing at the nurses' station was a girl with tied-up dark brown hair. His stomach gave an uncomfortable squeeze. *Please don't let it be...*

She turned around, her eyes widening and

her face falling as the same recognition that he was experiencing evidently washed over her.

'Oh, here he is.' Luan, one of the regular staff nurses, waved. 'This is Dr Woodhouse, Clara. Josh, this is our new Georgie.' She winked at him. 'I was just telling her all about your sister.'

Joshua kept his expression as neutral as possible as he walked forward and extended his hand. He hadn't exactly been friendly last night; his mind had been on other things. It had taken an age to settle Hannah back down after the car alarm had jerked her out of her sleepy state.

The woman was tall, slim with dark hair and brown eyes. She was dressed smartly in black trousers, a bright red shirt, flat shoes and her white lab coat. He tried to stop his gaze fixating on her high cheekbones and bright red lips. She was pretty—more than pretty. Something he'd failed to register last night in the dimly lit car park. 'Dr Connolly, I presume?'

Had he really just said that? Darn it. She was Scottish too. Would she think he was making a fool of her and mimicking the famous quote *Dr Livingstone, I presume?*

But, all credit to her, Clara Connolly gave a little tug at the bottom of her bright red shirt then held out her hand to his. Her handshake was firm—a little too firm. Maybe she was still annoyed about last night.

'Yes, I'm Clara,' she said, then her lips turned upwards as if someone had just reminded her to smile. 'Nice to meet you.' Was she nervous?

Okay. Those words were definitely said through slightly clenched teeth. He was going to have to make the best of the fact that he'd totally forgotten his new doctor was moving into his sister's flat last night. He didn't even know if Clara had known that he lived in the same building. Well, she did now. And probably thought he was one of the rudest men on the planet.

There really wasn't much recovery from this at all. He decided to get straight down to business. 'Let me show you around and tell you how we do things here,' he said, gesturing for her to follow him down the ward.

He was proud of his department and the reputation for excellence that it held. He was always very careful about recruitment, taking up multiple references in order to get a good idea of whether someone would fit in appropriately with his team. This time he hadn't had that opportunity. The job swap had happened so fast. He'd seen her CV, of course. It was impressive—as was the list of hospitals she'd worked at throughout her career. He'd even recognised the names of some of her supervisors, all colleagues he respected. He knew Clara was at the same stage of her career as his sister—but what he didn't know was what she was made of. It irked him; he couldn't help it. Qualifications were all very well, but could he trust Clara Connolly to fit into his team? This woman with the dark brown hair and brown eyes almost seemed as if she'd tricked her way in here.

She pulled a pair of glasses from her white coat and slid them on. They were red-rimmed, with a cartoon character on the legs. He pretended not to notice. He wondered if red was her theme. 'This is our general admissions assessment unit. We have fourteen beds. We don't leave kids in A&E; they come straight up here once they've been triaged and had any X-rays that they need. Ultrasounds can be performed on the ward, and we have a system where they get anaesthetic cream put on their arms downstairs, so if we need to take bloods up here we can do that straight away. If they don't need anything, we just wipe it back off.'

Clara gave a nod. He handed her an electronic tablet from a stack on the wall. 'You should have received a passcode this morning.'

She nodded and he pointed at it. 'We keep

all records electronically, and order all tests this way too. You can log into any device at any point in the hospital.'

He looked around the ward and kept walking. 'We have a general surgical ward, a medical ward, a twelve-bed paediatric oncology unit for treatments, and six paediatric beds in ITU—all on this floor of the hospital. You'll be expected to participate in a number of our paediatric clinics, all based on the ground floor, and carry a paediatric arrest pager.' He cleared his throat a little and spun around, lowering his voice. 'I see from your CV that you have experience in all these areas. I take it you're happy to cover them here?'

There was an edge of challenge in his tone, and one of her eyebrows gave the slightest hint of lifting. She tilted her chin towards him. 'I think you'll find I'm competent in all areas, Dr Woodhouse.'

'Well,' he said slowly, 'we'll see.'

'And just what does that mean?' There was a flash of anger in her eyes and she planted one hand on her hip.

'Exactly what I said. We'll see.'

He could tell she was trying to rein her anger in. 'I don't like the implication. I'm sure you can tell from my CV that I'm more than competent at my job. Anyone who knows me, or has worked with me, could also tell you that.'

He started walking towards his office. 'Well, that's just it. I don't know you and I've never worked with you. I've just had you thrust upon me without much warning.'

Clara had kept pace next to him as he'd started moving again but stumbled for a second over his last sentence.

She kept quiet until they were in his office but, before he had a chance to do anything else, she closed the door firmly and leaned against it, folding her arms.

'Why don't you tell me exactly how you feel then, Dr Woodhouse? Is this how you treat all your new starts? Because I hate to break it to you, but you really need to work on your welcome.' She paused for a second then glared at him. 'In both your personal and your professional life.'

For a second he was stunned. He'd been prepared for some comeback, but it seemed that Clara Connolly gave just as good as she got.

This might actually be interesting. He liked working with people who were straight talkers. It saved time.

He sat down in the chair behind his desk. 'This is my department, Dr Connolly. And I'll run it my way.' As much as liked her direct approach, he needed to make sure she knew who was boss.

'I'm surprised you have any staff at all.' The words shot out of her mouth and then she blinked. Was that a flash of regret in her eyes? Now they were out of the ward environment and he was looking at her full on, he could really get a sense of her. There were a few fine lines around her eyes, a smattering of freckles across her nose and she was wearing impeccable make-up. Maybe it was the make-up that kept drawing his gaze to her dark brown—currently stormy—eyes. Her bright red lips matched her glasses. And her hair—tied in a high ponytail—was bouncing as she spoke.

He took a breath. 'I wasn't familiar with the job swap policy. I hadn't even heard about it until Georgie told me she'd matched with you and was moving for six months.'

Clara looked him square in the eye. 'Any idea why she wanted to leave?'

He flinched. He wasn't quite sure if it was sarcasm or a genuine query. He ignored the remark. He hadn't told a single person the real reason Georgie had left.

'I normally recruit staff into the department myself. I like to make sure they're the kind of people who will fit into the team. I didn't get that opportunity with you.'

'So, what is this? A "go back where you came from" speech?'

Josh could think of a hundred things he wanted to say right now, none of them very professional. He hadn't been entirely himself these last few weeks, and even he could reflect that he might be taking out his frustrations about his sister's quick departure on the people around him.

Was he actually being fair to this doctor? At first glance, she was smartly turned out, punctual and appeared interested in the role. Should he be looking for more right now? He'd already gathered she'd had a long journey and her arrival at the apartment hadn't exactly been smooth.

He stared at her for a few moments longer. She seemed happy to wait out the silence—there was no compulsion to fill the gap with panicked words. It was almost like a stand-off.

He cracked first but kept his voice steady. It didn't matter that this woman had already annoyed him. It didn't matter that he couldn't quite decide how he felt about her challenging attitude. It really didn't matter that her light, unusual perfume was weaving its way across the room towards him, or that now he'd actually stopped for a few seconds he realised just how pretty she was. None of that mattered at all. He had a department to run.

'No. It's not a—as you put it—a "go back where you came from" speech. It's a "wait and I'll tell you how you'll fit in with my team" speech. Everyone who joins is supernumerary the first week. Watch and learn our systems. From next week, you'll be on the on-call rota like everyone else. Get to know the staff. Say hello to some of our more regular patients. If there are any procedures you haven't done in a while—speak up, ask to observe again. Familiarise yourself with them. Feel free to spend the day with the paediatric surgeons if you want to. Visit our day surgery unit and introduce yourself. Dr Morran, our paediatric oncologist, will have a whole host of protocols she'll want to go over with you, to ensure you can handle any emergency in her absence. Hans Greiger is our chief paediatric anaesthetist and our go-to for NICU. Make yourself known to him. By the time I hand you the page next week, Dr Connolly, I expect my patients to be in good hands. I expect you to be wise enough to identify the gaps in your skills to function in this role and find your own learning opportunities in the next week to increase your competencies.'

It might sound harsh. The truth was, at this

stage in her career he didn't expect her to have many gaps in her knowledge. But he treated every member of staff who worked in his department the same. He was a strong believer that all medics should be able to identify and seek out learning opportunities where they could. They were responsible for their own learning. He wanted a team to be able to reflect on their skills, and to know where their limits were.

She stayed remarkably silent. It was almost as if she'd expected something entirely different. Instead, after a few moments, she folded her arms across her chest and gave him a half-smile. 'Fine.' She paused and took a breath. 'Now, are we going to talk about the elephant in the room?'

He almost wanted to spin around and check behind him to see if one had just escaped from somewhere and actually appeared. She was still half smiling, and he recognised the tension in his muscles that had probably translated to his face. She knew she'd rattled him, but from the gleam in her eye he just wasn't quite sure that she cared.

'What do you mean?'

Her head gave a tiny conciliatory nod. 'I mean, we obviously got off to a bad start last night.'

Hmm. *That* elephant. 'You could say that.'

'Are you that mean to all the new tenants?'

'Most new tenants don't park in my space or set off a car alarm and wake up my sleeping child.'

She held up one hand, 'First—those parking spaces are ridiculously small. I probably did you a favour. How on earth could you have got your kid out of the car if you'd parked there?' She didn't wait for him to answer. 'But you're right, and I'm sorry. What's wrong with the lights down there? Are you all just supposed to fumble around in the dark? It's hardly safe. I couldn't see a thing and didn't know the car parking spaces were numbered until you came down the ramp in your car and the whole place lit up like a Christmas tree. Don't worry, I won't make the same mistake again. Was your little one okay?'

She was babbling again. This time it was his mouth that turned up in a half-smile. The more she spoke, the quicker she got, and the thicker her accent became. He shook his head. 'Hannah settled back down once I got her upstairs. Hope you didn't damage the car though; Len Brookenstein inspects that thing on a regular basis. It's basically his surrogate child.'

She pulled a face and sighed. 'Great. No, I didn't. At least I don't think so. It was just a cardboard box containing some clothes. And it barely touched his car. The alarm must be extra-sensitive.'

She was looking him straight in the eye, but the smile still dancing around her lips told him that they both knew the box had hit with a thud.

She shook her head again. 'Honestly, I did check—not a mark.'

Joshua frowned. 'Didn't Georgie leave you keys?'

Clara fumbled in her pocket and pulled out a familiar set. 'Yeah, but what's that got to do with anything?'

He stood up and stepped closer. 'And you didn't have these on you when you were in the garage last night?'

Her nose wrinkled. She tilted her head up to his. 'No, why?'

He touched her outstretched palm, turning over the cream plastic fob that was on the key chain. 'This is the sensor for the garage. If you drive your car down the ramp, or exit from the lift, the sensor automatically activates the lights.' He couldn't help but give a grin. 'And no, you're not supposed to—' he met her gaze '—fumble around in the dark down there.'

A little colour flooded her cheeks and she quickly tore her eyes away from his and looked down at the keys in her palm. 'Darn it,' she said as she lifted her other hand to turn the cream fob over. The movement made her fingers momentarily brush against his and a little shiver shot down his spine. He pulled his hand back. Recognition was obviously dawning. 'I just left the keys upstairs last night.'

'You didn't lock the door of the flat?' he asked incredulously.

'No.' She shook her head. 'Why would I? I was just planning on carrying all my boxes up in the lift. Doors and keys would just get in the way.'

He took a step back. 'I hate to break it to you, but you're in London now, Clara. You leave the flat—you lock it.'

She frowned. 'But isn't there supposed to be a guy at the entrance—a concierge? People can't just wander in.'

Josh rolled his eyes. 'I kind of assumed that you might have picked up on the fact that most of the residents in the building call our concierge 'the happy wanderer'.'

Clara was still frowning. 'What do you mean?'

'You haven't met Louie yet?'

She shook her head.

'Ah, then let's just say, Louie doesn't much like sitting behind a desk. He's officially retired and took the concierge role after his wife died because he didn't like being in the house by himself.' Josh gave a smile. 'He likes to chat. If you can't find him, it's because he's chatting somewhere. It doesn't do much for the security of the building, hence why you shouldn't leave your door open.'

Clara looked as if she wasn't quite sure what to say. He guessed she was already feeling sorry for Louie, even though she hadn't met him yet. 'Does he get into trouble for that?'

Josh shook his head. 'No one has the heart to complain, and he's really obliging. He'll accept deliveries for you, sort out any issues in the flat, let repair men in if you need them and supervise if necessary.' He glanced out of the window for a second as a few memories surfaced in his brain. 'He tells Hannah great stories. She's his biggest fan.'

Clara's voice was hesitant. 'Hannah—is that your daughter? The kid I saw last night?'

The question gave him a jolt and a flash of annoyance again as he remembered how the car alarm had jerked Hannah from her sleep. 'You mean the kid you woke up? Yes, that's her.'

Clara wrinkled her nose. 'Sorry. Just an accident. I'm sure it won't happen again. Hope she didn't keep you and your wife up all night.'

It was like a bucket of cold water being dumped all over his head. It had been a while since someone had made a casual comment about a wife or partner around him. Most people that knew him were well aware that his wife had died years before. His mouth opened to automatically form the words 'I'm a widower', and then he stopped. He hadn't invited this woman into his life. He still had no idea if she'd be much of a team player. The old feelings of irritation washed over him. He didn't need to share personal information with her. It was none of her business.

He didn't even form a reply, just picked up a file that one of the secretaries had left for him containing induction paperwork for Clara. 'Here,' he said. 'This is yours. There's a million online training courses you need to complete—health and safety, manual handling refresher, anaphylaxis etc. HR want you to complete some of this paperwork and drop it off. They're on the top floor. There's an office across from here that you can use—and introduce yourself to Helen, my secretary, and Ron, the ward clerk. They can pretty much tell you everything else you need to know.'

He moved behind her, catching a whiff of that perfume again as he opened the door. It was nice, unusual. But her words had irritated him. He didn't want to have to explain his situation to this new doctor. Not when he'd seen the flash of sympathy in her eyes when he'd told her Louie the concierge was a widower.

It was an odd thing when that familiar flash in someone's eyes sent all the hairs on his arms in an upward prickle. He didn't want pity. But for the last five years he'd seen it time and time again. He'd rebuilt his life, focusing on Hannah. He was busy at work, with most evenings spent taking Hannah to a wide variety of activities—none of which she seemed to want to stick at.

There wasn't a place for sympathy in his life. He and Hannah were good. They were solid. Plus, he didn't want the naturally inquisitive and uncomfortable questions that sometimes followed from the widower label being revealed. As he'd reached for the door handle he'd glanced at his hand. He'd taken his ring off two years ago. It had been the right time and right move for him.

Not that'd he'd met anyone serious. Sure, he'd dated. Georgie had encouraged him, babysitting Hannah on occasion. But there had never been anyone who gave him that… spark…that thirst and curiosity to find out so much more about them. Maybe there would never be.

If Abby had lived, he liked to think that their marriage would have endured and they would have grown old together. It wasn't that he didn't think future love wasn't a possibility; it was just that no one he'd met seemed to fill that space.

'I'll leave you to get on with things,' he said briskly to Clara as he strode out of the room. He had intended to take her with him on this introductory ward round. But he needed to get away. She had enough to be getting on with, and so did he.

Clara stared at the broad back striding away from her, and wondered what on earth had just happened. When she'd spun around and seen her new boss she'd tried her best not to let her chin bounce off the floor.

Typical—Mr Grumpy. He didn't like her at home, and it was clear he didn't like her at work. Clara had always shot straight from the hip. She'd hoped London would be a fresh start. But already things were rapidly going downhill. It didn't help that she'd hardly got a wink of sleep last night. Maybe it was being in a new bed, or maybe it was the unfamiliar creaking. What certainly hadn't helped was the low background noise from outside. The restaurants and bars had seemed far away when she'd been on the balcony, but in the middle of the night the raucous laughter and shouts had drifted all the way up to her room. That would teach her to leave the balcony door ajar.

A guy behind the desk gave her a wave. 'Clara?' he asked.

She nodded. 'Come over here,' he said, 'and bring your file. I'm Ron.' He pointed to his badge. 'Some people call me a ward clerk—' he lowered his voice '—but other people call me a magician.' He pointed to the seat next to him. 'I have coffee and doughnuts and I can help you with your paperwork and your on-line learning.'

A friendly face. Thank goodness. She smiled and walked over. 'Coffee would be great, thanks.'

She sat down next to him, spending the next hour completing the necessary paperwork and flying through the online learning packages. Ron printed her a pocket-sized list of hospital extensions she'd need, along with a reminder of people's names. He also seemed to know everyone's schedules and could tell her where to find the people she wanted to introduce herself to.

He ran down the list as only someone who'd

worked in a place for years could. 'Hans Greiger. Fantastic. Has encyclopaedic knowledge of superheroes and always speaks to kids about their favourite hero as he's sending them off to sleep. In ICU he's so up-to-date with his research. The unit here has trialled lots of new life-saving interventions. Dr Morran, the oncologist, is similar. Research is a big thing here. Dr Morran has two teenage kids of her own and coaches rugby.' His eyes sparkled and he held a finger up. 'She's the tiniest woman you'll ever meet, but she could take someone down twice her size. Now…' he pulled over another list, running his finger down it and pointing at various names '…he gets cranky if he hasn't eaten. She always has a book in her coat pocket. Marlon can make balloon animals for kids—always handy to know. Fi— she can find food anywhere. If you're hungry, ask Fi. The cupboards might look bare, but she'll spirit some food from somewhere. And if you're phoning for a scan try and get Ruby. She's the most obliging.'

Clara nodded as she listened, writing the occasional note. Ron was clearly a mine of information. She bit her lip and hesitated for a second 'Er…what about Joshua? You didn't mention him.'

Ron gave her a surprised look. 'Best guy on the planet. Without a shadow of a doubt. Shame he's never met someone. He deserves to.'

'What do you mean?'

Ron frowned. 'Georgie didn't tell you? I thought you two had been in touch and swapped houses and things.'

'We have. I mean, we did. But she didn't mention her brother at all. I didn't even know he lived in the same apartment block...' she lowered her voice '...and that turned out well.' Ron raised his eyebrows and she shook her head and gave a smile. 'Forget it. And the apartment—it's some place. Absolutely gorgeous.'

Ron nodded. 'Yeah, when Georgie first moved in, she couldn't stop showing us all pictures of the place. She felt so lucky. She and Joshua both inherited money from an elderly aunt. Turns out she'd a huge nest egg from something her late husband had invented that no one had known about. Georgie and Joshua were stunned. But it all worked out in the end. At least Josh doesn't have to worry about a mortgage alongside everything else.'

Another curious comment. She tilted her head slightly. 'What do you mean?'

Ron gave the smallest shake of his head. 'I

just assumed Georgie would have mentioned it. Josh is a widower. His wife died a few weeks after Hannah was born; he's brought her up on his own.'

Her skin turned cold and she groaned and thudded her head down on the desk, putting her hands over it. 'Oh, no.'

'What?' asked Ron.

But Clara hadn't quite finished thumping her head on the desk as her stomach gave a whole array of uncomfortable twists. That explained the look on his face. She had almost seen the shutters banging closed across his eyes and hadn't for the life of her understood why. Darn it. Georgie might have mentioned it.

Ron nudged her. 'Okay, new girl, spill. What have you done?'

Clara pulled her head up, well aware that her hair was now all mussed around her head. 'When I got into the flat last night it was a series of disasters. I ended up in the pitch-black car park, parked in Joshua's space, spilling my clothing everywhere and then setting off a car alarm as he was carrying his sleeping daughter to the lift.'

Ron cringed but shook his head. 'Okay, poor start agreed, but what's that got to do with Josh being a widower?'

She closed her eyes tightly and silently pointed to the office at the side. 'When we were in there, I mentioned the bad start between us last night. I might have said…' and she paused, dying a little inside '… I might have said that I hoped it didn't take long for him and his wife to settle Hannah back down.'

Ron sat back, hands outstretched on the desk in front of him. 'Oh,' he said slowly, pulling a face. He paused for a few seconds, then gave a tentative reply. 'Well, you weren't to know.' He turned to face her. 'But Josh never said anything?'

She shook her head and put her hands back over her face. 'He just kind of shut down. Told me to get on with things.'

She pulled her hands back and stared down the ward. He was nowhere in sight. 'I should apologise,' she said, pushing herself up. But Ron was much quicker.

'Oh, no,' he said, shaking his head and putting one hand over hers. 'You shouldn't mention it. I know him. I know what he's like. Take a breath. File the information. And, please, don't do it again.' She met Ron's gaze and could see a whole host of emotions written all over his face. Pity, wariness but, above all, sincerity.

'Really?' She felt uncomfortable. Her first

reaction—the one she usually acted upon—was to apologise. 'I don't want to get off to a worse start than I already have.'

Ron's eyebrows lifted so high they practically merged into his hairline and this time he gave her a half-smile. 'Seriously?'

She let out a nervous laugh. Ron pushed another doughnut towards her and she shook her head. 'No way. I can't afford to buy a new wardrobe of clothes. I need to get my bearings and find a gym nearby.'

Ron put his hand on his chest. 'And this is why you have me. There's a gym in the hospital, free for staff, though it's used for patients during the day. But there's also a fancy gym in your apartment block, and a swimming pool. Didn't Georgie tell you?'

Something clicked in her brain. 'Oh, it might have been on the house swap details. But, to be honest, once I saw the view from her flat I stopped reading.' She tapped her fingers on the desk. 'I'd like to say that I wish I had an ancient rich aunt but, honestly, I didn't love the place last night.'

'Really? Why not?'

'Noise,' she said simply and then shrugged her shoulders. 'I live in a cottage in the middle of nowhere. The only noise I ever hear is a hooting owl or the baaing from the sheep in the next-door field. London? Well, that's a bit different. And it's warmer down here. At least it feels that way to me, so last night I left the door open on the balcony to let some cool air in.'

Ron let out a laugh. 'And instead you got the fun and pleasure of Canary Wharf and the docks?'

She sighed and pushed her glasses up on her head and rubbed her eyes. 'Something like that.' She stretched her back. 'Maybe it was just the bed, or the unfamiliar creaks. But, whatever it was, I felt like I hardly slept a wink.' She leaned on the desk. 'And, between you and me, a no sleep Clara is a cranky Clara.'

'I'll file that as a warning,' said Ron and pulled a large envelope from the drawer next to him. 'Here, take your things upstairs to HR. At least then you'll know you're getting paid at the end of the month.'

She slid her paperwork into the envelope and stood up, catching a glimpse of Joshua again. He was talking with another doctor at the end of a patient's bed. Her stomach flipped. Was it odd that the boss hadn't taken her on his ward round to get them used to working together? It had kind of been the norm wherever else she'd worked. First ward rounds were generally a mine of information on a colleague's work style. As she watched him talk seriously with someone else she wondered if she should be offended.

Every ounce of her felt uncomfortable. Maybe he doubted her competencies since he hadn't had the chance to select her himself? She'd never had her competence questioned before; she prided herself on being a good doctor.

But he'd mentioned team stuff too. Had the debacle last night meant he'd already judged her, and she'd failed? Did he think her personality wouldn't fit with his team? What on earth did that say about her? Was she awkward? Unlikeable?

So much uncertainty. And so *not* what she needed right now. Nothing like making her confidence slip all the way down to her boots. Or, in today's world, her comfortable shoes.

She looked down and wriggled her toes in the American shoes her friend had introduced her to. She now had them in six colours. Nothing else would do for long days on her feet, and in a job where she could literally walk for miles.

She took a deep breath. The first nurse she'd met, Luan, had seemed really nice. And Ron was obviously the font of all knowledge ere. They didn't make her feel as if she didn't fit in.

She stared at the names on the list in front of her. Would all these people like her too? Maybe her directness would be her downfall. She'd never had to adjust her personality type to a job before, but there was always a first time.

She looked up again, just as Joshua looked up from his end of the ward. His forehead creased and she turned away quickly before he scowled at her again.

Ron caught her reaction. 'Best not to say anything,' he reminded her. 'It's been a few years, but I doubt he wants old wounds reopened. It's not exactly a good first conversation to have with your boss.'

She swallowed and nodded, painting a smile on her face. 'Yes, of course. You're right.' The envelope crinkled in her hand. 'I'll take this up to HR then start trying to meet some of the people on this list.'

Ron nodded as the phone started ringing. She walked away as he picked it up.

Although she'd been tired this morning, she'd still been enthusiastic about starting a new job. But in the last two hours all that enthusiasm had slowly drained from her body. Maybe this had all been a big mistake.

As she walked along the glass front corridor she stared out at the London skyline.

Why on earth had she wanted to leave home?

CHAPTER THREE

CLARA HAD KEPT her chin up. First, she'd learned to sleep with the balcony door closed. Second, she'd spent hours at the hospital meeting, and hopefully charming, everyone on the list Joshua had given her. There had been no problems. She'd practically memorised Dr Morran's protocols. She'd familiarised herself so completely with the staff of Hans Greiger's ICU that she knew what they all took in their coffee. But it was worth it. Even though she was officially supernumerary, she was still allowed to work and assist if appropriate. It meant that Hans had been around when she'd intubated a small baby and put in a central line. Two tricky procedures, particularly on a small child. She knew he was observing her— he probably did that with any new doctor at her level, but she'd felt her heart swell in her chest when he'd not only complimented her on her skills, but also how she'd dealt with the family.

Thirdly, she'd also managed to spend a bit of time in day surgery, and she'd met the physios, occupational therapists, speech and language therapists and dieticians who were all assigned to paediatrics. The only thing that had appeared tricky was the electronic systems. Occasionally she'd found herself logged out, irritating when she was in the middle of ordering tests or chasing results. She'd called the IT help number and asked them to get back to her. It wasn't a problem she could solve on her own.

By the end of the first week she was exhausted, but also slightly relieved. Her time felt well spent. She'd only caught an occasional glimpse of Joshua at work, and none at all at home. The only downside of the week had been the complete obliteration of the 'chocolate drawer' at home—but at least she'd found the gym. It had good equipment, excellent views and she'd only seen one other person in there. Perfect. Sweaty and breathless wasn't her idea of socialising.

Today was her first official staff meeting—something that Joshua did on a daily basis. She was interested to see how it went.

Ron nodded her into the kitchen when she arrived. 'Get coffee. Kettle is boiled.'

She glanced at her watch. The staff meeting started at seven-thirty and it was only seven o'clock. He gave a gentle shake of his head. 'They're all already in there.'

She gulped. 'Did I get the time wrong?'

'No. It's just how they are.'

Her feet were itching to race into the room. Her cheeks already felt warm with embarrassment at being the last to get there. But she took a breath and headed into the kitchen, filling her cup with coffee and a splash of milk. The meeting was due to start at seven-thirty. She wasn't late—and she wasn't going to act as if she was.

She pulled her shoulders back as she walked the few steps over to the meeting room. Her hand wavered, wondering if she should knock, but then she tilted her chin upwards and opened the door, keeping her back straight as she glided into the room with a smile on her face.

Joshua was midway through talking. He stopped and glanced over at her, irritation evident. 'Oh, good, you're here. Sit down and we'll continue.'

'Continue?' Clara glanced at her watch. 'I didn't think we were due to start for another...

twenty-seven minutes. Did you forget to tell me about the time change of the meeting?'

She kept her voice light, but her words were carefully chosen.

One of the other docs in the room snorted into her coffee. She lifted her cup to Clara. 'Welcome, and I like you already. I'm Lucy and, if you don't know it yet, these morning meetings are like a race to see who can get here first.' Lucy looked at Joshua. 'Although the boss usually waits until everyone is in the room.'

Lucy connected her gaze with Joshua's frown and stared him straight in the eye. There was an unspoken implication there, and Clara appreciated it.

She sat down in one of the chairs. 'Well, I'm sure if I've missed anything significant Dr Woodhouse can fill me in later.'

There were a few seconds' silence and then Joshua shifted on his chair before he started speaking again. The meeting went quickly and was over in thirty minutes. Joshua briefed the staff on a product recall, new dosage instructions for a drug used commonly in paediatrics, sick leave cover and alerted them to a few patients he wanted closely monitored. Dr Morran followed up, highlighting a few of her own patients with special instructions.

Other members of staff jumped in with general information about delayed results, special consults awaited from other areas and new admissions. Now Clara knew why Ron had told her to bring coffee. The amount of information crammed into that thirty minutes was huge, but crucial for a safe, smooth-running department.

She scanned the room, putting names to faces she hadn't met yet. Her phone vibrated in her pocket and she tilted it sideways to see who it was. Ryan. Guilt swamped her. She hadn't really had a chance to have a real conversation with him since she'd got here. They'd left messages, but kept missing each other. She knew there had been a complication about him moving out of her place—and she had emailed Georgie an apology—but the reply had been short and sweet.

No problem. These things happen.

She wondered what Ryan was making of the mysterious Georgie. Everyone here talked about her with real affection. She couldn't help but hope her colleagues back in Scotland had been a bit more friendly than Joshua.

'Dr Connolly?'

She jumped at the stern-sounding tone,

embarrassed that her mind had wandered off while the others were leaving the room.

But, before she got a chance to respond, her pager sounded in her pocket.

She glanced at the pager. 'Duty calls,' she said with an uncomfortable smile on her face, before disappearing out of the ward towards the stairs.

As she hurried down the stairs to A&E she wondered if she'd already got herself in trouble. The doctor in A&E had asked her to attend. She already knew that the protocol stated that all children got fast-tracked up to the assessment unit, so they weren't left in the A&E environment which could, on occasion, be stressful for children. But Clara liked to have a little faith in her colleagues. If an A&E consultant was asking for the paediatric page holder to attend, then she would go.

She pushed through the swinging doors and made her way to the nurses' station. Joe Banks, a guy she'd met briefly the previous week, gave her a wave. 'You on call?'

She nodded.

'Good. I've got an unusual one for you; feel free to ask for a second opinion.'

Clara flinched, wondering if he was questioning her skills. But her rational brain made her take a deep breath. The guy had barely met her. If this was an unusual case, it wasn't strange to ask for a second opinion.

He pointed to the screen in front of him and pushed a chart towards her with his other hand. She scanned the screen. A seven-year-old girl with fever, tachycardic and itchy rash. It could be any one of a hundred things, and not that unusual a case.

Joe lifted his hand as if he'd read her mind. 'Wait until you see the rash. I've put this kid in a side room meantime, until you decide if she's infectious or not.'

Ahh… Now she understood. If the triaging doctor in A&E thought a child could have an infectious disease, they wouldn't send them up to the assessment unit. That could result in a whole host of other children and relatives becoming exposed to whatever virus they carried.

Clara picked up the notes and gave him a smile, 'Thanks,' she said as she walked towards the side room. Outside were some basics—gloves, masks and aprons, along with hand sanitiser. For an airborne infection, masks like these weren't effective, but old habits seemed to die hard. Clara used all the equipment provided and went in to make her own assessment.

'Hi there, I'm Clara, the paediatric doctor.'

She smiled at the anxious-looking mother and the little girl, who was lying sleepily on the bed. 'I'm going to ask you a few questions and take a look at Jessica, if that's all right with you.'

The woman nodded. 'I'm Meg.' Her eyes ran up and down Clara's body. 'Should I be wearing those?'

Clara shook her head. 'We're not even sure if Jessica has anything infectious yet. If she does, we'll take the right precautions.'

She proceeded with a list of questions, gathering the background and history of Jessica presenting at hospital today. She also asked Meg a few questions, checking to see if she was pregnant, or if she, or any other members of the family, had any symptoms of their own. It was all just precautions. Some infectious diseases spread easily between close contacts, and some were risky if a woman was pregnant.

Once she'd asked all her questions, she re-checked Jessica's temperature, her heart-rate, and gently removed the hospital gown to get a better look at the rash.

Her pager sounded and she glanced down to where it was clipped to the pocket of her coat. The number was for the ward upstairs. She had a horrible feeling in the pit of her stomach that someone was checking up on her.

There were so many conditions that this could actually be—measles, meningitis, or even just a viral infection. Although some rashes were distinctive, many—in the early stages—were indistinguishable. As she kept examining Jessica she turned over one of the palms of her hands and stopped, turning back. There, on the side edge of her hand, was a strange mark. Clara leaned a bit closer. Was that a bite, or a scratch?

Either way, the area around it was slightly red and inflamed. It wasn't completely obvious, and could easily be missed.

'Do you have any pets?' she asked Meg.

Meg nodded. 'Two cats, an ancient tortoise and a rat.'

Clara gave a small nod in reply and made some notes. 'First of all, I'm going to prescribe something for Jessica to bring her temperature down, and then I'm going to order some tests. I'll try and ensure they happen as quickly as possible. Let me do that, and then I'll come back and talk to you again.'

Meg gave a half-smile, looking semi-relieved. Something was flickering in Clara's brain—a condition she'd only seen once before. She wanted to check some of the details before she asked any more questions.

It was odd. She absolutely knew that she

had to rule out all the normal things that could cause a fever and rash. The list was almost endless, but something deep down inside her was just telling her not to ignore that tiny bite mark.

She'd seen a case before of a disease caused by a rat bite. But she had to check the details. She had to be sure.

A voice appeared at her back. 'What's the problem down here?'

Her muscles stiffened. She hadn't even had a chance to chart her preliminary findings. Last thing she wanted was her new boss looking over her shoulder while she ordered some unusual tests.

'Don't you realise that all children go straight up to the assessment unit? It's a well-known fact that A&E environments can cause unnecessary stress for both children and their families.'

She bristled, trying at first to bite her tongue, and then deciding to just go with how she felt. She spun around, keeping her demeanour entirely professional. 'Of course I know that. I'm not some half-ass student. If I'm keeping our patient down here, I have an entirely good reason to do so.'

He flinched, obviously not expecting her answer to be so direct. But he was acting so pompous, talking to her as if she were some kind of inexperienced idiot. She heard a gentle cough next to them both and turned to see Alan Turner, the head of A&E, raise one eyebrow and give her a half smile.

She tried to restrain her flare of anger back into a less flammable state. 'Don't worry, Dr Woodhouse,' she said quickly. 'If I need your expertise I'll be sure to let you know. Everything is under control.'

Joshua stared at her, long and hard. She could almost see his brain whirring, trying to decide whether to reprimand her or leave it for the time being. He glanced sideways at Alan, who was pretending not to listen to them both—even though he clearly was.

'I expect to hear from you soon,' Joshua said through clenched teeth.

'Of course,' she said with an enforced breeziness in her tone and watched as he spun around and strode down the corridor so fast he looked as if he might break into a sprint.

Alan moved over next to her, looking down at the forms in her hand. The blood test she'd been looking for hadn't appeared on the IT system—probably because it was so unusual, so she'd written the order by hand.

He made a surprised nod. 'Haven't seen that one before.'

She pulled an uncertain face. 'I know it's a long shot. But I have seen it before, and my gut is just telling me to check.'

Alan glanced back down the corridor. The door at the end was swinging from where Joshua had just disappeared. 'You do know that any test like that—I mean one that's completely unusual for our lab—has to be signed off by the Head of Department?'

Clara's heart sank. Her fingers crumpled the form a little. 'Please tell me you're joking.'

He shook his head and pulled the slightly bent form from her fingers. 'I'm not so sure that now's a good time to go chasing after Josh,' he said carefully.

'Me neither.'

Alan gave a slow nod. 'Okay, so let's just say that on this occasion I'll sign it off for you. I'll be interested to see what comes back. Let's just call it professional curiosity.'

Clara heaved a huge sigh of relief. She hadn't realised any unusual requests had to go through the Head of Department. It made sense. Sometimes inexperienced doctors could order a whole host of expensive tests that might not be necessary. This was the NHS. They had to be careful of costs and she understood that.

She knew that Alan signing off on this test

might cause friction between him and Joshua at a later date. She held the form close to her chest. 'Thanks, Alan, I appreciate this.'

He held up his finger as he moved away. 'It's a one-time-only deal.' He looked back over to the swinging door again. It was clear he'd sensed the friction between her and Joshua. She'd need to think about that. It wouldn't do for other areas to think that staff in Paediatrics didn't really get on. 'Just until you get settled in,' said Alan as he gave her a nod and disappeared behind a set of cubicle curtains.

Clara sighed and looked at her forms again. *Please don't let this be a wild goose chase,* she prayed.

Joshua was trying so hard not to explode. Yes, he was a control freak. Yes, he always had been. And no, that didn't always work well for a Head of Department.

But he also tried to mentor his staff. He wasn't the type of doctor to leave a colleague without support, or in a situation they couldn't handle.

But somehow he knew Clara Connolly wasn't that type of doctor. He'd been asking around. Paediatric circles were surprisingly small. Everything he'd heard about her in the last week had been reassuringly, but annoyingly, good. He couldn't quite understand why this attractive woman seemed to irritate him.

Just her jaunty, slightly lopsided ponytail seemed to annoy him.

When he'd known she'd been called down to A&E he'd hung around the ward, wanting to check up on the assessment notes she'd written. It wasn't intrusive exactly—just a way of reassuring himself that he could trust her skills. But neither the patient nor the notes had appeared. And eventually he'd run out of patience and gone down to the A&E department. He might have been just a little snappy with her, but her response had been equally snappy and not one he would expect from a new start doctor.

He'd had to bite his tongue. Georgie's voice had echoed in his ears as he stormed back up the stairs to Paediatrics. Would he have checked on her? Of course not.

How would he feel if he'd been in Clara's position and someone had checked up on him?

But, ultimately, all paediatric patients who were admitted were his responsibility. He had a right to ask questions. To check up on his staff.

He waited an hour. Then another hour. His fingers were itching to check the electronic record, but he stopped himself.

'Any word from Dr Connolly?' he asked.

Ron looked up from the computer. 'Just to get her a tuna sandwich from the canteen when I'm going. She's caught up in A&E.'

She'd been there for more than two hours. This was getting ridiculous.

No. He wasn't going to wait a minute longer.

When he reached A&E five minutes later he could see how busy it was. Alan Turner was walking out of Resus and pulling off a pair of gloves. He fell into step alongside.

'Josh, twice in one day? I didn't realise we'd paged you.' He was smiling, but Josh could tell from the words and tone that he knew exactly what was going on. He gave Josh a tiny nod. 'Your new colleague—I like her. She's smart—I would never have picked up on that case.'

Josh's footsteps faltered. Both men knew exactly what he was thinking. He bit his lip then asked the question. 'What case?'

Alan gave him a knowing smile. 'Rat-bite fever.' He shook his head. 'What a call.' He walked into the nearby treatment room and started washing his hands. Josh couldn't help but follow him. Rat-bite fever? He'd never even heard of it.

'I had to look it up' Alan smiled. 'But the diagnosis has just been confirmed.' He pulled a bit of a face. 'Oh, apologies, I signed off on the test for her.' He waved one wet hand. 'You weren't around.' He paused for a second and then added carefully, 'I told her not to bother you.'

He was lying; Josh knew he was lying. He liked Alan. He respected Alan. But he wasn't about to stand by and let the Head of another department conspire with a new member of his staff—at least that was what it felt like.

He kept his voice steady. 'I'd appreciate if you didn't do that again, Alan.'

The implication was clear and as Alan grabbed some paper towels to dry his hands he gave a conciliatory nod. 'Sure.'

It was a truce. Alan had successfully let Joshua know that his staff member had performed well, while equally trying to keep him in check.

The annoyance that had been flooding through Josh's veins had diverted slightly, but not disappeared completely. He would have expected Clara to give him a call and update him, particularly around an unusual case. But he couldn't help but be impressed that his new doctor had diagnosed a condition he'd never even heard of.

He pulled out his phone, ready to look it up,

just as Clara walked out of the nearby room, a wide smile across her face.

'Oh, Joshua,' she said. 'I was just about to call you.' She waved back towards the side room. 'I know you like to treat children on the assessment unit, but I've just started Jessica on some IV antibiotics. She's got streptobacillary rat-bite fever. I'm worried about septicaemia.'

He lifted the chart from her hands and scanned it before picking up a nearby tablet and pulling Jessica's file. Clara's cheeks flushed and she pulled a piece of paper from her pocket. 'My notes. I'm a bit old-fashioned. Haven't put everything on the electronic record yet—just her obs and what I've prescribed. It seemed more important to get the antibiotics started once I had the diagnosis.'

The words prickled down his spine. 'How did you manage to run a test like this without my sign off?' It didn't matter that he knew the answer to this question; he wanted to see what kind of excuse she gave.

As she moved he caught a waft of something. He had no idea what kind of perfume she was wearing, but it was like a shockwave to his system. It reminded him of a garden after a rainstorm—sweet, sensual and enticing. It was delicious.

He blinked and breathed in, letting the scent

permeate his body. For a second all he could focus on was the smell. He'd never had a re-action like this before to a perfume. Every female colleague that he worked with wore a different scent. All were indistinguishable. But this? This was entirely different. He looked up. Clara was talking. He could see those signa-ture red lips moving. But for a few seconds he couldn't concentrate.

The noise in the busy A&E faded to a dull hum. There was a roaring in his ears, as if parts of his brain were awakening after they'd been snoozing for the last few years. His eyes focused on Clara's eyes. He could see a tiny flare of panic in them. Her voice started to permeate. 'So, I know it wasn't the usual turn of events, but this case, it wasn't usual either. I knew time was of the essence and the lab test takes a few hours. It seemed im-perative to rule it out as soon as possible. As I was with her, the petechial rash changed— it became more pronounced around the bite wound. She started to experience rigors and a headache and joint pains.' She licked her lips and stopped talking for a second, pausing to catch her breath.

The roaring in his head hadn't stopped. His eyes couldn't move from hers. There was something about them. Not the colour. Not the mascara on her dark lashes. Something in the depths of them.

He had to stop this.

He held up one hand. 'Dr Connolly. Let's draw a line under this. Don't do it again. If you want to run specialist—and very expensive—tests, run it past me first. NHS is public money. I like to keep a check on things. As Head of Department that's my right.' He took a breath, 'If, however, I'm not here, then I'm fine with you running it past, for example, Alan. But *only* if I'm not at work.'

Right now he wanted to walk away, to try and sort out what was wrong with his head. But his professional mind was listing all the things he should be doing right now. Supporting his team member. Reviewing the patient. Ensuring the correct diagnosis had indeed been made. He also didn't want to admit that he was dying to pull his phone out of his pocket and read exactly what rat-bite fever was.

He spoke quickly before Clara had a chance to start babbling again. Why was she babbling anyway? Was she nervous around him? Worried he would give her trouble for going behind his back and ordering tests? He didn't need to say the words out loud—they both knew that was exactly what she'd done. Once, he could let go—particularly when Alan might have been encouraging her—twice would be a reprimand.

'Why don't you introduce me to the patient and her family? I'm interested to see Jessica and make arrangements to get her upstairs. Maybe I can do that while you finish your notes?'

She twitched. And he wondered if the words he'd meant to sound helpful had actually sounded as if he was implying she hadn't done her job. He waved his hand towards her. 'Dr Connolly?' He gestured towards the side room.

She gave a nod. 'Sure, follow me.' And she walked ahead, leaving a trail of enticing scent for him to follow.

He smiled to himself as the children's story of the Pied Piper who'd lured children away by playing music came floating into his head. This wasn't exactly music but it felt close enough, and he shook himself as he followed the trail that she'd laid.

CHAPTER FOUR

THINGS FELT AS if they were settling down. She'd been here a month. The noises from inside the flat and out were annoying her less and less. She'd managed to familiarise herself with all the regular staff at the hospital and her first few on-call shifts had gone well. Children always came in overnight so she'd decided just to stay when she was on-call overnight, sleeping in a comfortable room next to one of the wards.

Joshua was always in promptly the next morning to review all new admissions and seemed to grudgingly agree with all decisions that she'd made. She couldn't pretend it wasn't a relief.

Since their first few encounters she'd more or less managed to stay out of his way. But he was a curious kind of guy. Any staff member she met seemed to love him. Unlike most hospitals, people at the Royal Hampstead Free

Hospital seemed to work here for years, not quite as transient as other places she'd worked in, and most of the regular staff had nothing but praise for Joshua.

On several occasions she'd come across him sitting with a child. Playing a game with them. Laughing with them. Reading a book to them because he'd sent a weary parent to grab something to eat and they didn't want to leave their child alone.

Clara had done the same herself on many occasions—she loved those moments with the patients—so she wasn't quite sure why watching him from afar, rubbing a kid's hair as they fell asleep against him, had tugged at her heart in a way she didn't want to admit.

It had been six weeks since she'd started her meds and she definitely felt a little better, not quite so flat as before. She'd registered with a GP here in London, who'd asked her to come in when she needed a repeat prescription.

Her GP had been lovely and readily acknowledged the stress and strains on fellow doctors. She'd offered to also refer Clara to one of the counsellors in the practice and Clara had surprised herself by accepting.

Now, as she pulled her legs up on the chair she'd positioned next to the window at the balcony, she could finally admit to starting to like this place just a little. Sure, there were no sheep banging their noses against her bedroom window, but sitting here watching the sunset spill orange and red light over the water was pretty mesmerising. She cupped her hands around her mug of coffee and reached for a biscuit. There was beauty here, and she wanted to take the time to recognise and enjoy it.

Now she was starting to feel a little better she could recognise that the incident back home with the toddler, Ben, had been the trigger for her. It wasn't always like this. Sometimes depression just seemed to sneak up out of nowhere; other times, there was some kind of event or trigger that started her down that path. The truth was, it was likely that depression would always be in her life.

A noise at the door made her jerk, spilling coffee down her jumper. She sat up as the main door to her flat opened and a sleepy-looking child walked inside clutching a book in one hand and a card in another.

'Auntie Georgie,' she murmured, blinking her tired eyes.

The words made Clara's limbs unfreeze from their automatic defensive position. She jumped to her feet and moved quickly across the room. Her brain was working overtime. Had she left her door ajar? No.

The card in the child's hand was a slim key card—the same that opened the door to the flat. Hannah. This had to be Hannah.

Clara dropped to her knees in front of the child. 'Hannah?' she said gently.

She wasn't quite sure if the little girl was sleepwalking or not. She knew better than to suddenly wake a child who was sleepwalking.

The pale-faced little girl blinked. Her eyes were slightly glazed. She was wearing pink and white pyjamas covered in the latest trendy cartoon character and was clutching a popular kids' book with a bear and a group of kids on the front. Her fine brown hair was mussed. It was clear that at some point she'd been sleeping.

'Hannah,' Clara said again softly, not wanting to startle her, but clear that somewhere around here Joshua Woodhouse would be in a state of panic.

She gently took the key card from Hannah's hand. It made sense that while Georgie lived here Hannah had gone freely between her aunt's flat and her own. But now? The thought that Joshua Woodhouse owned an entrance card to the flat she was currently staying in left her feeling a little odd. Invaded even.

She looked over at the phone and realised she'd no idea what Joshua's phone number was. She scanned her brain. Was the whole apartment block a bit like a hotel? Could she just dial someone's flat number to get them on the phone? Then she groaned. Of course not. All the flats had A, B, C and D after them. She squeezed her eyes closed for a second, willing the number of the space she'd parked in downstairs on the first day to spring into her head. Nope. Nothing. She couldn't even guide Hannah back up in the lift to her father's flat.

'Book,' said Hannah, holding out her book to Clara.

She hesitated, then took it from Hannah's hand, leading the little girl gently towards the comfortable sofa that was close to the nearby phone. As soon as Clara sat down, Hannah climbed up onto her knee and settled there, pulling the book down in front of them both.

Now Clara was torn. She wasn't sure that Hannah was actually sleepwalking. Maybe just not yet fully awake? She opened the first page of the book and had a brainwave. Louie. What had Joshua called him...the happy wanderer?

She picked up the phone and dialled, sighing with relief when Louie answered. 'What can I do for you, Dr Connolly?'

She spoke quietly. 'Thank goodness. Louie, Hannah Woodhouse has just wandered into my flat. I don't have her father's phone number and can't remember the flat number either. Do you have a way I can contact him? He must be out of his mind. She seems really sleepy and I don't want to startle her awake.'

Louie gave an easy sigh. 'Ah, let me do that. Hannah used to go easily between the two homes. Give me two minutes and I'll get a hold of him.'

Clara put down the phone, breathing a sigh of relief. Hannah nudged her. 'Story,' she said in a still sleepy voice, leaning back and laying her head on Clara's shoulder.

It was such an easy move for the little girl, as if she did it every day, and it made the breath catch in Clara's throat. There was an aching familiarity about this little girl.

The heat coming from her body as she sat in Clara's lap seemed to permeate right through to her soul. She'd thought about having kids for a long time. She'd even made enquiries a few months ago about using a sperm donor and having IUI.

Part of her had wondered if it was just how she was feeling, so she'd stalled on the decision. But, even now she was beginning to feel better, the loneliness in her remained, seemed fastened to her in every way.

She'd spent many a long hour and restless

night with kids on the wards. She'd seen the tears, the temper tantrums, the heartaches and the pain. She didn't have an unrealistic view of what being a parent would be like.

But, as this little girl sat on her lap and urged her to turn the pages of her book, Clara couldn't help but wonder if this was what life could be like. There were always tiny doubts niggling in her brain. Could a person with depression really be a good single parent? Would her mood ever affect her relationship with her potential child? No matter how many doubts she had, just this simple act was filling her with hope.

She started to tell the story in a quiet voice. The words had a rhythm to them, making it easy to get into the swing of the short story. Within less than two minutes they were almost at the end and Hannah's head was nodding, as if she were falling completely back asleep.

The door banged open and Clara started. Joshua stood in her doorway, his face dark with rage. 'What are you doing?' he demanded, striding in as Clara put her finger to her lips.

She took a deep breath, trying to ignore the way her heart was thudding erratically against her chest at the initial fright. He'd crossed the room in a few long strides and stood towering over her.

She refused to let herself be intimidated. 'Shh,' she said quite openly now, nodding towards the sleeping Hannah, who'd been unperturbed by the banging door.

Joshua opened his mouth and then stopped, clearly collecting himself. Clara waited. She tried to put herself in his position—realising Hannah was missing from their apartment and being thrown into a blind panic.

She couldn't imagine how terrified he'd been, and she tried to reassure herself that his blundering into her apartment was just the reaction of a panicked father.

She kept her gaze locked on his and nodded to the space on the sofa beside her.

He paused for a second and then sank down next to her, his sigh of relief audible.

'I guess that Louie never got you,' she said in a low voice.

'Louie?'

She nodded, her hand rubbing gently at Hannah's back. 'I phoned him when Hannah appeared.' Her gaze didn't waver. 'I didn't know your phone number, or your mobile number. And, despite you drawing my attention to the fact I'd parked in your space that first night, I couldn't remember that number either, so I couldn't bring Hannah back up to you. I had no way to get in touch with you, Joshua, and, to be honest, I wasn't quite sure if she was sleepwalking or not. I didn't want to startle her.'

Joshua had the good grace to break their gaze as a sheepish expression flooded over his face. He let out a low curse. 'I'm sorry, Clara. I'd put her to bed, went in to check on her after a phone call and she was just…gone.'

He ran his fingers through his rumpled hair. 'My heart almost stopped. The door was open, and I hadn't even noticed.' He thumped his head back against the sofa and groaned. 'My five-year-old walked out of the flat and I didn't even notice,' he repeated. 'What kind of a crap dad am I?'

She could almost see the breakdown happening—see the pieces of the puzzle slotting into all the worst-case scenarios he could imagine—as he sat next to her. She reached over and tapped his hand with hers. 'She's fine. And she's lovely, by the way.'

For some reason Clara didn't move her hand from his.

He shook his head. 'No, Louie didn't get me. He'll probably appear up here any moment to make sure everything's okay.'

Clara nodded. 'At least you knew to check

here first.' Her eyes glanced towards the key card for the entry panel to her flat. 'I take it Hannah used to come up and down between you both?'

Joshua sighed. 'Yes. She wasn't ever supposed to use the lift by herself and she did know that. But often she would ask if she could come down to Georgie's, or Georgie would phone and say to send her down. Then one of us would either go up and down with her, or put her in the lift, and the other would meet us at the door.' He took a long, slow breath. 'But on a few occasions, particularly around bedtime, Hannah would sneak down to Georgie's.' He gave Clara a smile. 'Apparently my sister's story-telling skills far outweigh my own.'

'I'll keep that in mind,' said Clara, then raised her eyebrows at Joshua. 'We should really talk about you having a key to what, essentially, is *my* flat right now.'

'Ah…' He bowed his head a little just as there was a knock at the still open door.

They both turned their heads. Louie caught sight of the scene, clocked Hannah still in Clara's arms and gave a slow nod. 'Just checking all was well. I'll be back downstairs.' He gave Clara a knowing smile.

Before either had a chance to say anything, he'd disappeared again.

It took her a few seconds to realise that she still had her hand on Joshua's and she pulled it back. It was odd—having him here in her place. At work he was her boss. Here, he was someone entirely different—a worried parent. And the first man she'd had in the apartment—invited or not.

Joshua leaned forward, putting his head in his hands and squinting a sideways glance at the sleeping child in Clara's arms. 'I sometimes think I'm making a complete mess of all this,' he said.

Clara blinked. She hadn't quite expected the admission. 'Why do you think that?' she asked cautiously.

He raised one hand. 'Well, first off, I have a child who wanders out of our place and down to a relative stranger's apartment, climbs into her lap and apparently asks her to read her a story.'

Clara nodded but gave a loose shrug. 'Exceptional circumstances. I'm not entirely sure if she realised I wasn't Auntie Georgie.'

'Oh, she knows,' he said. 'She's been asking when we could come down and meet you.'

'She has?'

He nodded. 'I told her it wasn't appropriate.

That you were a new workmate and couldn't be expected to have us down here.'

'Seems a bit tough.'

'You think?'

She nodded. 'I don't mind. You could have just asked, you know.'

He pulled a face but didn't answer.

'You said first off. What's second?' It might be intrusive to ask, but he'd started the conversation and she could see that now he'd relaxed around her a bit he did seem as if he wanted to talk. Maybe she could finally get to see the man that everyone at work told her about.

He leaned back again. 'Secondly, I have a daughter who seems to start a million activities but doesn't want to stick at any one of them. She gets bored within a few weeks and wants to quit.' He sighed. 'I don't like to complain. But I just get my schedule to fit around one thing then she wants to swap to another. She's tried ballet, gymnastics, baton twirling, Brownies and tap dancing so far.'

Clara wrinkled her brow. 'And you've let her quit everything?'

'Shouldn't I?' A worried expression crossed his face.

She gave another shrug. 'Well, it is up to you. You're the parent. But maybe you should try something different.'

'Like what?'

She took a few moments to consider before she replied. 'Let's think about an activity which could be an essential—swimming, perhaps.' She adjusted her position on the sofa so she was facing him a little better. 'That's an activity you wouldn't want her to quit. Safety—every parent wants their child to be able to swim.'

He gave a slow nod. 'Okay...'

'Okay, so you tell Hannah that she's going to start swimming lessons and it's really important. You let her know that she'll probably be going for a few years, and that she can't stop until she can swim up and down a big pool.' Clara was thinking back to her own swimming lessons as a kid. She gave a careful shrug. 'Of course, there could an occasion where she doesn't gel with a particular instructor, and you might swap her to someone else.' She held up her finger. 'But you let her understand this is a non-quit activity. You let her know this is important.' She looked out of the window at the orange setting sun. 'You tell her that once you know she can swim safely the two of you can have lots of fun on holiday, somewhere with a big pool.'

His eyes narrowed a little as he thought

about her idea. 'You think I should try something like that?'

Clara nodded. 'I'm not a parent. And I must have had a different temperament as a child, because once I started something I became a bit obsessed about it. But lots of my friends were like Hannah,' she said reassuringly. 'They tried lots of things over the years.'

She reached a hand out again and touched his arm. 'You know, this has to work for you too. It can't be easy having to change your schedule all the time. Maybe some kind of stability would be good for you both.'

'Are you saying I don't offer Hannah stability?' He was instantly on edge and sat up straight with a flash of anger in his eyes.

Clara let out a sigh and shook her head. 'Why are you so defensive? Why is everything I say a fault?' She rubbed Hannah's back again, enjoying the way the little girl was snuggled into her. 'If I didn't see this gorgeous little girl on my lap, and know you must be finding this tough, I'd think you hated me, Joshua Woodhouse.' She gave a sad smile as he flinched. 'Maybe you're just not used to someone who talks as frankly as me—and calls a spade a spade.'

He waited a long time before he spoke. He

gestured with his hand between them. 'I don't do this.'

'Do what?'

'Talk about things… Talk about being on my own with Hannah…. Talk about how I wonder if I'm doing things right all the time.' He leaned forward and pressed his hands into his face. 'Talk about if I'm letting her down.'

'You're not letting her down.' The words were out instantly. 'Why do you think that?'

She could see something flit across his eyes. Guilt. Doubt. This was clearly a man who felt he'd let someone down before. The first person to enter her head was his wife. He was a widower. No one had really told her any details. She just knew his wife had died from some kind of terminal disease just after having Hannah. Why would he think he'd let his wife down?

He hadn't answered and she tried to push past what she'd just seen in his eyes. 'You put too much pressure on yourself, Joshua. Every friend I've got who's ever had a child spends their time endlessly worrying that they're getting it wrong. Haven't you realised yet that the whole world is just muddling through?' She gave a little laugh. 'Even the ones who have pre-made meals for a month and a huge blackboard with everything written on it in their kitchen.'

Joshua's face relaxed into a smile and he visibly shuddered. 'Okay, I've never done that.'

'See?' Clara smiled. 'You're not doing too badly then.'

There was something nice about seeing him a little more relaxed than normal. He seemed to settle into the contours of her sofa. 'I'm sorry you got a fright tonight,' she said. 'Why don't you give me the number of your flat, and your mobile number, so if Hannah ever appears again I can let you know where she is.'

He pulled a face. 'It won't happen again. I'm sorry. Keep the key card. I shouldn't still have it. Of course I shouldn't. To be honest, I'd just forgotten about it.' He looked at his daughter and Clara's heart panged at the clear look of love in his eyes. 'I'll talk to Hannah tomorrow. I'll tell her she shouldn't come down here.'

Clara shook her head. 'You don't need to do that. She's welcome to come down here if I'm in.' She gave him a smile. 'To be honest, I liked the company. London's kind of lonely. And it was the best book I've read in ages.'

'You're finding London lonely?'

'Kind of. You know, we're in a busy hospital, it's a busy city, you can't turn around without bumping into someone but...' she let

her voice trail off for a second while she collected her thoughts '... I miss my best friend,
Ryan. I miss my old cottage with the sheep
that press their faces up against the window.'

Joshua let out a loud laugh. 'What?'

She grinned. 'Text Georgie; she's been there
over a month. She'll know all about it by now.'

His smile stayed for a few seconds, then
faded. 'I guess Hannah's missing her auntie.
She spent a lot of time here. Georgie was Hannah's partner in crime; the two of them used
to gang up on me.'

Clara raised her eyebrows. 'Sounds like a
job I could embrace,' she said cheekily. 'No,
honestly, she can come down any time. If you
think she needs to hang about with a female
for a while or—' she chose her words carefully
'—if you need a break and I'm not working,
just give me a call.'

She could see the conflict in his eyes. Joshua
Woodhouse didn't accept help easily. He was
wavering. After a few seconds his eyes connected with hers. The setting sun was streaming oranges and reds through the glass across
the room. It was like being held in some kind
of spell. Her breath was stuck somewhere inside her chest. It was the first time in for ever
that she'd felt some kind of connection with
someone.

And she knew it was ridiculous. Joshua was her boss. And, apart from work, she didn't think they had anything in common. But seeing him like this—exposed, worried, vulnerable—it was a far cry from the confident, smooth consultant she saw at work. This was a normal guy. One who was juggling a million balls in the air and trying to stay afloat. Maybe she hadn't given him enough leeway. Maybe she'd been too quick to take offence at some of his words.

'That's a really kind offer,' he said. His gaze hadn't left hers. It was steady. And though it was only a few words, it felt like so much more.

He paused then added, 'My nanny left around the same time as Georgie and my short-term replacement isn't working out as well as I would have hoped.'

Clara nodded. 'Well, think of me as another option. It's not a problem.'

She wasn't sure if this was her imagination or not, but she could swear there was something in the air between them. A weird kind of buzz. A smile danced across her face. There was something nice about this, relaxing. There hadn't been much opportunity, between the two of them, to have some quiet time like this. The hospital was so busy—and she found him so frosty at work—that they'd been like ships passing in the night.

Her heart gave a little skip as Hannah adjusted herself on Clara's lap. Clara swallowed, wondering if she was mixing up her feelings about motherhood with what she sensed in the air between her and her boss. That could be dangerous. And confusing.

But Joshua was still looking at her. She wasn't imagining that. And, as his face started to crinkle into a smile, she was sure she wasn't misreading the flicker of attraction in his eyes. She'd never pried into his life before. She hadn't felt the urge. But all of a sudden she wanted to know everything.

'And if you ever need an emergency babysitter for on-calls, remember, I'm just down the stairs.'

He stood up and leaned close, her nose catching the spicy scent of his cologne as his arms entwined with hers to pick up Hannah. For the briefest of seconds the tiny scratch of stubble on his cheek brushed against hers and she sucked in a breath, feeling her eyes widen as they met his.

His hand and arms were against the curves of her body as he grasped his daughter and he halted for the briefest moment. For a second their lips were mere inches apart and she wondered if he was going to kiss her. From this close she could see the tiny flecks in his blue irises and just how long his lashes were—completely unfair for a guy.

'Thank you, Clara,' he said huskily in a voice that seemed to ripple over her skin.

'Any time,' was her automatic reply.

He pulled back, lifting Hannah from her arms and heading out of the door of her apartment back to the lift. Her legs took a few seconds to move and by the time she reached her own door she only had a chance to give a brief wave.

'Got to stop meeting like this,' she whispered as the smooth steel doors slid closed.

Her heart was thudding in her chest as she shut her own door and leaned against it. Had that all really just happened?

She drew in a few quick breaths as she crossed the room, pausing to pick up the abandoned storybook still sitting on her sofa. Her hand ran over the back of the sofa, feeling the warmth from where Joshua had been sitting.

This *had* really just happened.

She kept moving, sitting down on the modern cream chaise longue next to the balcony and pulling up her legs to her chest. Part of her felt warm and fuzzy, matching the glow streaming in from the sunset outside. But part of her was a little muddled.

She'd started to feel a bit better—about everything. Work, the change of scene, her life, and what the future could hold.

Spending time with Hannah tonight had cemented something in part of her brain. She definitely wanted to be a mother. Whether she had a man in her life or not, if it were possible, she'd love to have children in her future. But was it something she should pursue now, or later? She wasn't getting any younger. Treatments were tough. And expensive. She had to be realistic about things.

But should she really push away the chance of meeting a man she could love and spend the rest of her life with? Would any guy she met want to date a woman who was happy to go and do IVF on her own to have a child?

Things were so complicated. She didn't want to view any potential dates as father material. She wanted to keep things separate in her brain, and in her life. But was that realistic?

She leaned back on the chaise longue and sighed, letting the warm orange glow bathe her face in its dimming light.

For the first time in for ever she'd felt a spark of *something*. She hadn't even felt that when she'd been dating Harry six months ago. This was different. This was something that made her skin tingle, her blood pulse and the tiny hairs on her body stand on end.

It made her mouth curve automatically upwards.

Could it really be a 'thing'?

She let out a groan. She was going to have to exercise the thing she struggled with most—patience. And just wait and see.

Darn it.

CHAPTER FIVE

JOSHUA'S HEAD WAS in knots. One of his doctors had quit. Well, not actually quit. He'd had to leave due to a family emergency back in Portugal. But he'd made it clear he regretfully couldn't come back, and the space in the rota seemed to be multiplying by the second. Two others had been struck down by the norovirus which was currently storming its way through the hospital, their paediatric anaesthetist had chickenpox—so severe he'd be lucky not to be admitted to ITU himself—and one of his junior doctors was expecting, and it turned out she had one of the worst cases of hyperemesis gravidarum he'd ever seen.

His pager sounded again and he muttered, 'I swear, if that's someone else sick…'

'You'll what?' Clara appeared at his elbow, a smile on her face, even though he knew she was run ragged covering here, there and everywhere.

'I'll probably run and hide,' he admitted. 'We're too many staff down already.' He wrinkled his brow. 'Don't you have a clinic?'

Clara nodded. 'But Ron's contacted them all, and I'm seeing them up here rather than at the other side of the hospital. It means that I can keep an eye on the assessment unit too.'

Joshua stopped walking and looked at her for a second. 'Why didn't I think of that?'

Clara grinned up at him. He breathed in and it was a little shock to the senses. She was wearing that perfume again that reminded him of a garden after a rainstorm. It made him lose the ability to concentrate—hardly good for today.

They'd come to some kind of truce. He couldn't quite understand why she'd started off pushing all his buttons in the wrong way, but now he'd taken time to take a step back, be patient and leave his judgement unclouded, he actually quite liked her.

She'd been so good about Hannah, particularly when he'd burst into her apartment. The conversation that night had seemed to put them on an uneven balance—one that could easily teeter in one direction or the other.

But she'd rapidly proved herself at work. The rest of the staff liked her, and she seemed clinically sound. On the few occasions he'd brought Hannah into work, Clara had gone out of her way to chat to her and spend time with her. Auntie Georgie's flat had quickly become Clara's place, and he wasn't sure if he liked that or not.

But, more than that, she was just…there. It was as if his senses picked up whenever she was around. He could hear her laugh before he walked through a door, sense her presence in the ward before he ever set eyes on her. She was patient with anxious parents. Good with teenagers. Magical with the terrible twos.

His brain was trying to deal with the fact that he was enjoying her being around. Maybe it had been that first glance. The shock to the system, realising he'd noticed how attractive she was. The colour of her lips. The curve of her hips.

Sure, he'd dated a few women over the last year or so. But none that had been special to him. None that had given him that suck-in-your-breath-for-a-moment feeling. He'd kind of forgotten what that felt like and had thought himself incapable of feeling like that again.

Maybe it was his history. He'd got used to being on his own. It was hard to learn how to trust again when his trust had been so badly broken. It was harder still when he'd loved the person who'd broken his trust completely, and she had loved him. He'd thought he was over things; he was sure he was ready to get back out there. But the slightest hint that the person he was dating wasn't being completely up front with him was enough to send him in the other direction without a second's hesitation. It didn't matter that it was ridiculous. Everyone was entitled to their privacy. But he just couldn't shake off the underlying conviction that was buried deep down inside of him—a relationship meant no secrets, no lies. It wasn't just his own heart he had to protect now; it was Hannah's.

But Clara? She was dancing around the edges of those thoughts on a pretty permanent basis. Which was a shame, as she was only here for six months and there was no way he'd introduce a potential girlfriend to Hannah unless he thought she might be important.

So it was easier to keep Clara in a different kind of box—one where he didn't think about her that way.

But sitting on the sofa with her a few weeks ago had pushed hard at those boundaries. She was easy with the touching; it came so naturally to her. She probably didn't realise it had been a long time since someone other than a parent or his sister had touched his hand in that kind of way. With affection. With care.

Clara stopped walking, spinning around until she was facing him. 'You didn't think of it because your brain doesn't function that way.' She gave a good-natured shrug. 'You're a man. Multi-tasking is a whole new language to you.' She gave him a wink as she walked away. 'Anyhow, I'll never admit it was Ron's idea.'

He laughed as she disappeared through the doors. Clara was full of quips. And he liked that. He liked her sense of humour. It reminded him not to take life too seriously, and he needed that when some of the days here were tougher than others.

Half an hour later she was back, her expression serious. She didn't beat around the bush. 'Help,' she said quickly, 'I need a second opinion on a kid.'

He was on his feet in seconds. 'No problem—what's wrong?'

He started walking with her as she rattled off the child's symptoms and her suspicions. 'Lewis Crawley is seventeen months—temperature, abdominal pain, drawing his knees up to his chest, jelly stools, vomiting bile...'

He put his hand on her arm. 'Clara, stop. What is it? This sounds like a textbook case. Why are you worried? You clearly know what's wrong.'

She was the palest he'd ever seen her. Jittery even. Not the cool doctor who'd diagnosed a weird and wonderful disease in the first week he'd worked with her.

'I... I just want a second opinion. And we don't have our normal anaesthetist. Who will take the case? Who will do the surgery?'

Joshua stopped and put both hands on her shoulders. 'Do you know this kid?'

She shook her head, and he could see the gleam of un-spilled tears in her eyes.

He had no idea what was going on here. And he'd have to get to the bottom of it. But, in the meantime, if this toddler had intussusception and the bowel had telescoped inside itself it was a surgical emergency.

'Okay, let's see him.' The examination took moments. Clara was right with every call. He could see she was trying to keep her emotions in check, so he went back over things with the parents to satisfy himself that they understood what was happening. Then he contacted the surgeon on call for the day, and phoned an alternative paediatric anaesthetist.

Clara typed up the notes as he spoke, recording every extra detail. She'd done everything she could—even ordered all the tests and completed the emergency consent form with the parents.

On a normal day, Joshua would have given any colleague a second opinion and then left them to carry on. But this wasn't a normal day. And he wasn't going to leave her.

He waited until both the surgeon and anaesthetist had come up to the ward, and the theatre staff had appeared to take Lewis and his parents down to surgery, then he glanced around to make sure there were no eyes upon them, slid his arm around her shoulders and guided her into the nearest room, closing the door behind them.

The nearest room was the stationery cupboard, not the best venue for a discussion like this. He took his arm away and turned to face her. 'Okay, Clara, you did everything perfectly. Tell me what's wrong.'

She was shaking—her body was actually shaking—and he watched as she dissolved into tears, muttering a curse under her breath.

Her head was shaking, but her face was covered with her hands. 'I'm sorry,' she said. 'I just...' she took a deep breath and dropped her hands and her gaze '...panicked.'

The word struck him as odd for Clara to choose. She was a member of staff who'd proved herself clinically competent over the last six weeks, and panic wasn't something he'd seen in her before.

'Tell me why you panicked,' he said steadily. He had to unpick this. If she needed support, it was his job to offer it.

She leaned back against one of the shelves in the cupboard, taking a few moments before she lifted her dark gaze to meet his.

'I didn't expect this to happen.' Her hands were still trembling and instinct made him reach out and take one of them in his own.

'What happened?' His voice was almost a whisper, just willing her to continue.

Her eyes closed and she rested her head back. 'I had a kid, older than Lewis, back in Edinburgh. I wasn't at work.' She winced. 'I had norovirus.'

Just like today—two staff off with norovirus.

'By the time I got into work early the next day, I saw there had been a kid admitted overnight. He might have been a bit older, but the symptoms were all there. A locum had been covering for us and had dismissed intussusception and was querying a grumbling appendix and had ordered a scan for the next day.'

She swallowed and a tear slipped down her face. 'I knew what was wrong with him as soon as I saw him. We got him to Theatre as soon as we could, but…' she shook her head

'…part of his bowel was necrosed. Dead. He ended up with a permanent stoma.'

Pieces were slotting into place in Joshua's head. It didn't matter that this wasn't her fault or responsibility. What was important was how Clara *felt* about it. What it made her feel inside. They'd all had a case like this—likely, more than one. The *if only* aspect that tormented them in a way it shouldn't.

He gave an understanding nod. 'So, today?'

She gave a huge sigh. 'Today was the first case of intussusception I've dealt with since then. It just pushed buttons in me. Made me feel panic. Even though it felt textbook, I wondered if I was just making things fit because I'm just so scared of another instance getting missed.' Her head sagged and she pulled her ponytail out, shaking her head as if to give herself some kind of relief.

Her dark hair was mussed and full, scattering over her shoulders and around her face. Every time he'd seen Clara she'd had her hair pulled back in some kind of band or clip. He'd never seen it loose before and the effect was quite stunning.

His hand was still holding hers. She hadn't pulled away, but the trembling had finally stilled. He spoke slowly. 'You did a good job today, Clara. You saw a child and diagnosed him with a condition, and got him appropriate treatment. I'm always here for a second opinion. I'm always happy to do that—so don't be afraid to ask again.' He chose his words carefully, wanting to reassure and build her confidence back up. 'But you didn't need it today. Your clinical judgement was spot on. I have confidence in you. You've proved yourself since you got here. I've not heard one query about any of your work. Have a bit of faith.'

Her brown eyes looked up and their gazes locked.

'I understand it brought back bad memories. I get that we all have triggers.'

There was a moment's silence—so much unsaid. It was the first time he'd seen Clara vulnerable—just like she'd seen him when Hannah had disappeared from the flat. She'd been good to him that night, even though she'd really had no reason to be. After the frosty way he'd treated her he couldn't have blamed her if she'd called him out for not noticing Hannah leaving immediately. He would have deserved it. But she hadn't said a single word like that, just invited him to sit down and talk.

He wasn't quite sure how he'd ended up in a cupboard with Clara but, face to face, this was as close as they'd got. Her scent was wrapping its way around him, pulling him in like some magic power. He'd got to the stage now that whenever he got the slightest whiff of that scent he would raise his head to see where she was. There was something about being in a tight space with someone. Being so close that he could see the tiny beating pulse at the apex of her neck, the tiny smudge of foundation on her cheek and the way her red lipstick had started to wear away. He knew he was staring, but it didn't feel awkward or uncomfortable because he knew she was staring too.

He wondered what she was seeing. Could she tell that he was worried about her? Did she know that he trusted her clinical judgement? Would she notice the lines and dark circles around his eyes because he hadn't been sleeping well lately? The little patch he'd missed this morning when shaving? Or might she sense the fact that he still wondered if he was managing to fulfil the role of both mum and dad to his daughter? Hannah deserved so much love and attention. Sometimes he looked at Hannah and his heart swelled so much in his chest that he thought it might explode.

Clara blinked as she watched him then moved slowly, her other hand lifting and resting on his chest. 'Thank you,' she whispered.

It was in his mind in an instant—that immediate instinctive need to move just a few inches forward to close the gap between them. His eyes focused on her lips as she licked them and he had to root his feet to the floor to stop them moving. The heat from her palm was flooding through his thin cotton shirt, warming his chest and spreading outwards. But it was the inward sensation that was making his breath catch somewhere in his throat. In his entire life, he'd never wanted to kiss a woman so badly.

Was it the red stain still on her lips? The way her loose and mussed up hair look completely sexy? Not moving was currently a form of torture.

But then the spell was broken. Clara closed the tiny space between them, stepping forward, sliding her hand up around his neck and pressing her lips against his.

It was like a roar in his ears. All the brakes were off. He slid his hand through her thick hair and pulled her tight against him. She tasted sweet and as he breathed in the fresh garden scent filled his nostrils. One of his hands stayed in her hair while the other pulled her close to his hip. He could feel the curves of her body against him.

Clara Connolly wasn't afraid of kissing. She met him match for match, pushing him back against the shelves on his side. His hand moved, sliding under her white coat and brushing the skin where her shirt met her trousers.

She made a little sound—one of pleasure—and it nearly drove him crazy. It was as if their minds melded.

They both pulled back, breathing hard. Clara let out a little laugh and lowered her head. When she lifted her head back up her eyes were glowing. The warmth from that glow spread all across his skin.

'Should I apologise?' she asked.

He shook his head and let out a small laugh too. 'Should I?'

'Somehow I don't think we'll be the only hospital staff to share a rogue kiss in a cupboard.'

This time he nodded as he smiled. 'I don't think so.'

Clara reached up and grabbed her hair, pulling it back into the band wrapped around her wrist and then straightened her shirt. 'How do I look?' It was clear she was planning on heading back outside.

'Fine.' Was he disappointed?

Staff came in and out of this cupboard all day—the last thing he wanted was to get caught in here. The gossip would spread like wildfire. And, funnily enough, he'd never really been the type to have a clinch in a cupboard or on-call room—no matter how much hospital staff joked about it.

'Oh, wait a minute.' She stood up on tiptoe and wiped one finger at the edge of his mouth. 'I think I left my mark.' She pulled back her finger, examining the minuscule hint of colour. 'That's better.' She smiled as she put her hand on the door handle.

She paused for a second and he could see her taking a deep breath, composing herself. A little buzz of pleasure flushed through his veins. 'You wait thirty seconds,' she shot over her shoulder as she opened the door and stepped outside into the ward.

As the door closed he leaned back against the shelves again, laughing. He had no idea how that had just happened.

Well, no, of course he did. But his idea of trying to ignore the flare of attraction to Clara had obviously failed. A tiny part of his brain waved a red flag. He was her boss. He'd only guided her into the cupboard for some privacy because she was upset.

But Clara had made the first move and they were both consenting adults. Maybe she'd felt the same wave of attraction that he had?

He wasn't quite sure how he felt about that. Clara was only here for a temporary period. He had Hannah to think about. Maybe it was better to keep things neutral. Certainly at work that would be for the best. Last thing he wanted was for it to be common knowledge that something might be going on between them.

He nodded to himself and breathed, giving his face a quick rub to make sure there was no sign of her lipstick. He swung the door to the stationery cupboard open and stepped out onto the ward.

As the door swung back into place he jumped. Ron was standing—cool as a cucumber—behind the door. He lifted the cup in his hand and grinned. 'Made you a coffee. Here you go.'

And then he winked. And walked away.

CHAPTER SIX

SHE WAS DEFINITELY starting to feel better. The view from her bedroom window had stopped looking so alien to her. She'd started to enjoy standing on the balcony and listening to the sounds from below at night instead of pining for her view of fields with an occasional sheep's baa.

She enjoyed both the swimming pool and gym within the apartment complex, and Louie was practically her best friend. He even put her food deliveries from a supermarket in her apartment for her, taking care to put essentials in the fridge.

As for Joshua? She wasn't entirely sure what was happening there. A few more weeks had passed. She wasn't embarrassed at all by their kiss. It had sent a whole host of sensations whirling around her body. Most of all it made her feel alive again.

Joshua was hard to read. He wasn't avoiding

her. He didn't seem embarrassed either. But neither of them had even admitted the event had happened. Though, for some strange reason, it seemed to have helped break the underlying tension between them.

He was a bit easier around her, talking to her more like a friend, rather than a stranger who'd sneaked into his department. That, in turn, had helped her relax a bit more. She didn't need to prove herself at every turn. Three days ago she'd had another baby with intussusception, and this time she hadn't second-guessed herself—wondering if she was seeing symptoms that weren't there. The baby had been diagnosed by her in A&E, assessed by the surgeon and taken to Theatre within two hours of entering the hospital. All without any complications. She'd spent most of the next day hanging around little Abe and tickling his toes. For a baby who had required major surgery he'd been in a surprisingly good mood when he'd come around and made a rapid recovery, eating and drinking normally within a few days.

Joshua had appeared once or twice at her shoulder and given her a reassuring smile, but nothing more.

Part of her was entirely comfortable, and part of her had a longing for more. Her brain frequently told her that maybe he'd just been feeling sorry for her, but the cells in her body remembered his response. It hadn't felt like any kind of sympathy kiss—instead it had felt like a compressed well of passion. One that she wouldn't have minded exploring a bit further...

But she had taken one step forward. She'd finally pressed send on the email to the IVF clinic, making enquiries about treatment options and using donor sperm. It had felt monumental to her, even though it was a basic enquiry. Once she had all the information she could think again. And that made her feel good—good she'd made the decision, and good that she was thinking about what came next. Life wasn't just the place she was now; life was also the world of possibilities in front of her.

It was Saturday, and the day stretched before her. She was toying with the idea of being a tourist for the day. Buckingham Palace, Trafalgar Square, Tower Bridge and the London Eye were all on her radar. The weather was bright and sunny and there was something freeing about the thought of wandering for a while, maybe stopping for a bite of lunch and perhaps even a glass of wine.

She was just pulling on her jacket when there was a knock at the door. She pulled it open to see Joshua and Hannah standing outside. 'Something wrong?' she asked, glancing between them both. 'Do you need me to watch Hannah?'

Her first thought was that Joshua had been called in unexpectedly to work. Why else would they both be at her door?

'No, Auntie Clara. We're going to the Tower of London, and I want you to come with us.'

Clara was stunned but her face broke into an immediate smile. Firstly, at Hannah calling her Auntie, and secondly at being invited at all. Her gaze met Joshua's and he gave a good-natured shrug. 'I think my company alone is a bit boring for my daughter. She wanted to ask a friend.'

Clara knelt down so she was opposite Hannah. 'And that's me?'

Hannah nodded as if it was the most natural thing in the world. 'We haven't gone anywhere together yet and you've been here for *ages*.'

Her eyes gave the briefest glance to Joshua again. She wanted to be sure that Hannah wasn't pushing him into this. He might not really want to spend time with her at all. But the look in his eyes seemed sincere and half amused. 'What do you think? Have you been before?'

Clara picked up her bag and swung it over

her shoulder. 'Never. I'd just got ready as I wanted to do a bit of sightseeing today too. The Tower of London sounds perfect.' She pulled the door closed behind her. 'Thanks for the invite.'

Hannah started bouncing on her toes as they called for the lift. 'Told you she would come, Daddy.'

Joshua looked over as they stepped into the lift then leaned over and whispered in her ear, 'Prepare yourself. Hannah will talk *all* day.'

Clara gave a genuine grin. 'Can't wait.'

Because it was a Saturday they had to stand in a queue for a while to get through the entrance to the Tower of London. Hannah hadn't stopped bouncing and waited for her turn to get her picture taken next to one of the famous Beefeaters in their traditional dark blue and red uniform.

The inside of the Tower was busy, but they weren't in any hurry so enjoyed one of the tours, listening to the Yeoman Warder tell stories of the Tower's history, treachery, torture and legends. Hannah was captivated, particularly when they met the Ravenmaster and were able to hear the names of some of the ravens around the tower.

The queue for the Crown Jewels outside the

Jewel House in the Waterloo Block was large, snaking its way across much of the grounds. Joshua bought them all ice creams to eat while they stood and waited, entertained by a group of performers who re-enacted a few of the tales about the Tower.

As they moved forward into the dimly lit corridors towards the Crown Jewels Hannah slipped her hand into Clara's. For a second Clara was startled, but the little hand felt comfortable in hers and a smile slid across her face. 'Told you I was old news,' Joshua said in a voice low enough that Hannah couldn't hear.

Clara gave him a cheeky wink. 'Guess you need to up your game then.'

'Sounds like a challenge,' he said with a teasing tone.

'Not sure you're up for it,' she quipped back quickly. As the line moved forward, Clara lifted Hannah up onto her hip so she could get a better view of the Crown Jewels. They couldn't linger too long, as the line was constantly moving. But they got a chance to look at St Edward's Crown, which was used for the Coronation, and the huge Cullinan Diamond mounted in the ceremonial sceptre and rod.

Hannah's favourite was the Imperial State Crown with the huge Black Prince's Ruby set into the cross at the front of the crown, and she was delighted when Clara bought her a hand-sized replica of the crown in the gift shop later.

She toyed with the thin plastic box it was housed in, trying to stick her fingers through the tricky gaps. 'It's okay—' Clara laughed '—it's yours; you can take it out.'

Hannah sighed. 'But it's too little for my head.'

Clara nodded in agreement. 'It is, but you can sit it in your bedroom and look at it when you fall asleep. Maybe you'll have a dream about being a princess, or a queen.'

'Or a unicorn!' said Hannah excitedly.

Clara kept nodding but looked at Joshua in bewilderment. He laughed. 'You'll learn. It doesn't matter what the topic of conversation is these days, it always comes back to a unicorn.'

She shook her head. 'Guess I'm not as up-to-date as I thought I was.' Her heart was feeling full in her chest. She'd had such a lovely morning with them both. Playing the part of a tourist was always going to be fun, but doing it with them had made it so much better. They'd chatted easily today. Hannah was enthralled by the stories and the sights. Any hint of bad behaviour disappeared in seconds with the latest distraction.

As they walked out of one entrance to

view the blue and white Tower Bridge, Joshua's hand brushed against hers. He gave her a smile and then put his arm around her shoulder. 'Anyone hungry?'

'Me!' both Hannah and Clara shouted at once.

They strolled along the edge of the Thames until they came to a restaurant that had tables set out in the sunshine. It was obviously popular but, after a few minutes' wait, they were guided to a table and given some menus.

The waiter appeared as they were watching the tour boats on the Thames and took their order. Ten minutes later Clara was sipping a cool glass of wine and eating traditional fish and chips. She let out a sigh.

'What?' asked Joshua.

She smiled. 'Nothing—just a perfect day. Exactly what I wanted to do. I got to see one of the sights in London, and now I'm having a gorgeous lunch and a glass of wine.' She raised her glass. 'I thought I was going to be doing this by myself, so thank you for the invite today.'

Joshua's heart gave a strange kind of flutter in his chest. This morning he'd acted on a whim. Hannah had pleaded to invite Clara on their trip, and he hadn't let himself find a hundred reasons to say no.

Because he hadn't really wanted to.

He couldn't pretend that his stomach hadn't been giving the odd flip-flop as he'd knocked on her door. But Clara had seemed delighted. And his heart might have skipped a few beats.

All morning she'd been great company—attentive to Hannah, and easy around them both. They weren't dating, so there was no problem with her spending time with Hannah, but the truth was Joshua didn't really introduce any female friends to Hannah. He'd met a few of the fellow mums and dads from Hannah's time at nursery and now at school—children's party invites made that inevitable—but that wasn't a circle of people he would call friends.

Between working and Hannah's activities, there was hardly time to get to know the doctors he worked with, let alone their families.

Now, sitting here with the breeze from the Thames and the sun in the sky, Joshua realised for the first time in years he was actually enjoying himself.

As they ate their food he could see the excitement in Hannah's eyes. It had been there all day. All she wanted to do was impress Clara, and that made his heart ache a little.

Had he made a mistake? He knew she was only here for another four months.

Trouble was, Hannah had told him the other night how much she missed her Auntie Georgie. He knew she'd been angling to go down and see Clara instead and he'd made a kind of lame excuse. It wasn't even that he was self-conscious about the fact they'd kissed. He was much more self-conscious about the fact that last time he'd been in her apartment he'd more or less spilled out his insecurities about failing as a parent. He wasn't even sure why he'd put all that into words.

His mind had been on his sister too. Georgie had texted a few times, and he got the impression that more was going on in Scotland than she was actually telling him. He'd tried to call her and left a few messages. But they hadn't actually managed to talk in person for a few weeks. They were normally so close. He worried about her. He wasn't surprised that Hannah had said she was missing her auntie.

He lifted his glass of beer towards Clara. 'It's our pleasure to have you along with us today. We've had fun, haven't we?' He nudged Hannah and she nodded enthusiastically, her mouth full of pasta.

'I probably should have asked you before,' he admitted without thinking.

Clara gave a soft smile and met his gaze. 'Well, I'm just glad you asked now.'

The words and meaning hung in the air between them. For a few seconds the background seemed to fade away and it was just the two of them there. Joshua felt his mouth dry and his skin prickle. Clara's dark eyes were pulling him in, keeping him there. And he liked it. He liked it a lot.

Was Clara someone he could trust? Someone who would be truthful with him?

'Can we go to Buckerham Palace next time?' asked Hannah, her mouth still full of food.

It broke the spell and they both jerked. He frowned a little as he racked his brain. 'I think Clara might be working next week,' he said, but he gave Clara a warm smile. 'I'm sure we can work something out in the future.'

Clara nodded. 'I'd love to visit Buckingham Palace,' she said. 'It's definitely on my list.' She paused and bit her lip for a second. 'But I do have a day off this week. How about Hannah and I check out that film that everyone's been talking about? I'd love to go to the cinema and see that.' She leaned towards Hannah. 'I kind of need to take a kid with me, or people will wonder what I'm doing there.'

Hannah laughed and turned to him. 'Can I, Daddy? Can I?'

Joshua shifted in his seat. In truth, he didn't like being put on the spot. However, Hannah had been talking about this film non-stop and he had no idea when he'd finally get the time to take her.

'As long as it doesn't interfere with swimming lessons,' he said as he caught Clara's look of surprise.

'You started swimming lessons? That's wonderful. It's so important that you know how to swim.' She said the words to Hannah, but he knew her purpose was backing him up.

'I quite like it,' said Hannah quickly. 'Daddy got me a swimming costume with unicorns on it.' Her proud grin said it all.

Clara leaned forward. 'So what have you done so far? Have you held onto the edge and kicked your legs? Or have you been really brave and put your face in the water yet?'

'I did that last week!' shrieked Hannah.

'Wow.' Clara leaned back again. 'I am so impressed. I bet you'll be swimming without a float soon.'

Hannah nodded as the waiter came over to take their plates away. 'Any desserts?' he asked.

'Can I have ice cream?' said Hannah without taking a breath.

The waiter picked up the last plate. 'Better ask your mum.' He smiled at Clara.

Now Joshua really couldn't speak. No words would come out. He saw the instant that Clara sucked in a shocked breath. But she didn't speak either.

'Oh, that's not my mum,' said Hannah without a second thought. 'This is our friend, Clara.'

The waiter pasted a smile on his face and gave a wary and apologetic smile. 'So, who gets to make the ice cream decision?' he asked.

Joshua nodded quickly. 'Absolutely.' He looked at Hannah. 'Chocolate ice cream with chocolate sauce?' She beamed back and nodded.

The waiter disappeared and Joshua looked over at Clara. She still looked as though she was holding her breath. But there was something else—a tiny light of sadness in her eyes that he hadn't seen at any point all day.

He had no idea what that meant. But his heart seemed to give a twist in his chest. She looked sad. And he didn't like it when Clara looked sad.

It wasn't as if he hadn't experienced random people asking Hannah about her mother before. He'd learned to accept it was an easy mistake—even though it was tactless in this day and age, when families came in all guises. He and Hannah had spoken about this before when sensitive times came up—like Mother's Day. Hannah still had the simple reasoning of a child. Her mummy had died and was in heaven, next to the stars in the sky.

Those who did know her were supportive. Her teacher at school had asked her if she wanted to make a card for her auntie, her granny or her daddy on Mother's Day. These things were done smoothly, with no fuss, and Joshua appreciated that.

So, even though it had been a little awkward, he was surprised to see the hint of hurt in Clara's eyes. Was she just embarrassed by the comment? Or maybe it was something deeper. Maybe Clara didn't want to be a mum at any point. Maybe she couldn't have children. Or maybe she was hiding something else.

No. He pushed that thought away for now. Things had been going well. He had to try and move past the fact that Abby had kept secrets from him. He was jumping to conclusions. He couldn't assume that Clara would do the same. Whatever it was, he didn't want it to spoil their day.

'Another wine?' he asked her.

She gave a gentle shake of her head. 'I'm afraid I'm a bit of a lightweight. One glass is fine; two glasses make me feel a bit wobbly. Not my best time.'

He raised his eyebrows. 'Really?'

She smiled and nodded. 'You don't want to see it.'

'Maybe I do?' he teased as Hannah was presented with her ice cream.

All of a sudden he was struck with the thought that this day would come to an end, and he really didn't want it to. It was only early afternoon. He glanced over at one of the tour boats bobbing past. It was close enough to hear part of its guide's chatter. The guide pointed to a nearby hotel, naming it. 'It's for the rich, the very rich *and* the very, very rich.'

The people on board started laughing and Joshua looked over at Clara. 'Ever done the Thames tour?'

She shook her head. 'I've seen the boats often enough. They come right down to where the flat is.'

'There's a pier just near to here. We can jump on one of the sightseeing boats. They go right past the Houses of Parliament, and the London Eye. Want to give it a try?'

Clara pointed at one of the packed boats.

'It's definitely this kind of boat, and not the speedboat kind?'

They'd seen several of them shoot past in the last hour. Joshua laughed. 'Don't like the look of the speedboat tour?'

She gave him her best haughty glance. 'I'm just thinking about the bumpy ride. Wouldn't want Hannah to lose her crown, would we?'

He signalled to the waiter for the bill. 'Absolutely not. Just so long as you weren't scared.'

He was teasing her again and she seemed to like playing along. She slid her hand across the table to Hannah. 'Girls aren't scared. We're just far too clever to let ourselves get wet. Have you seen the people that come off those boats?'

Hannah squeezed Clara's hand and looked determinedly at her dad. 'Exactly,' she said in a voice that made him laugh out loud.

'Why do I feel as if you're both ganging up on me?'

Hannah gave a little nod as she slid her arms into her jacket. 'Because we are, aren't we, Clara?'

Clara grinned and gave him a wink. 'Absolutely.'

By the time they got back to the apartments Hannah was almost sleeping on her feet.

The boat trip had only been the start of the afternoon. They'd wandered around the shops for a bit, and come across a ticket booth with availability for some shows that evening. After a quick chat they'd gone for a musical about witches that Hannah had absolutely loved.

'I've always meant to take her to a musical,' said Joshua in a low voice as they waited for the lift. 'I just never got around to it.'

He smiled down at the slumped figure in his arms. 'You might have helped me create a monster. Now I'm going to have to take her to the ice one, the lion one, and the one with the genie.'

'I'm game if you are. Musicals are my addiction. I've always loved them. Did you see the way her eyes lit up while she watched?'

He gave a slow nod and the edges of his lips tilted upward into a sexy smile. She realised the first words that had come out of her lips and how they might have sounded.

I'm game if you are.

She couldn't help the low laugh that came from deep within her.

'You were saying?' he said huskily.

She stepped a bit closer and whispered in his ear. 'I'm not sure I should say anything at all. We have company.'

'I'm sorry I have my hands full,' was his quick retort.

She took a deep breath and looked at him for a second. They were flirting. After weeks and weeks of playing at just being friends, they were definitely flirting. And she liked this version of Joshua. He could be playful. And he could be deeply sexy. Probably not the best thought to have about her boss— who was also a single father—but she really, *really* liked it.

But something had struck at the heart of her today. She was a little bit jealous of the fabulous relationship he had with his daughter. It was something to aspire to. Would Joshua want to have more kids in the future? The offhand comment by the waiter had made parts of her pang even more badly than they had before.

She leaned against his shoulder. 'No, you don't,' she said honestly. 'You're lucky. And you know you are. You have a fabulous child, and you're doing a great job as a parent.'

He turned his head, his blue eyes locking with hers. His lips brushed against her forehead, sending a whole host of tingles shooting down her spine. 'Thank you,' he whispered. 'That means a lot.'

The doors slid open and Clara swallowed. Her floor was first.

'Do you want to come upstairs?' he asked, the words coming out so gravelly it sent a huge array of prickles across her skin.

Every single part of her wanted to scream yes. She knew he didn't do this—didn't ask women up to the apartment he shared with his daughter while Hannah was there.

But something was holding her back. If she closed her eyes for just a second she could imagine exactly what would come next. But did she want to cross that barrier between them? It could make things awkward at work. She, for one, wouldn't regret the next step, but what if he did?'

She pressed her lips together and swallowed before reaching over and touching his cheek lightly. 'I'm not sure that's a good idea. Hannah's had a big day. I'd hate if she was restless and saw something she shouldn't.'

Her stomach coiled. These words weren't entirely true. She really, really wanted to go upstairs to his place. And she felt sure. She just wasn't sure that he was.

Somehow even the touch of his skin beneath her fingertips let her know that she could fall hard and fast for this man, without him doing another thing. She was feeling good right now—her mood was better than it had been for months. Did she want to risk a chance of heartbreak? Particularly when this romance could potentially only last a few months. Her body felt ready to move forward, but did her heart?

She stood on her tiptoes for a second and brushed her lips against his. 'Thanks for a great day,' she whispered. 'How about we take a rain check?'

She could see the disappointment on his face, but he gave a slow nod. 'Of course,' he said smoothly as the doors slid open and she stepped out at her floor.

All the way to her door she wanted to turn back around and tell him that she'd changed her mind, but there was too much uncertainty there for her. Maybe they could chat about things in a day or so. It could be this uncertainty was only her head—she could well be reading too much into this. A short-term thing might suit Joshua. She just wasn't entirely sure it suited her.

As the door opened she bent to pick up a large envelope from the floor. Wrinkling her nose, she pulled it open as the lights came on around her.

A number of glossy information catalogues fell into her hand. The clinic. The clinic had sent her the information she'd requested. A small card slid out and she picked it up from the floor. A password and code to access the sperm donor catalogue.

Her skin prickled and her mouth dried. This had all suddenly got very real.

CHAPTER SEVEN

IT WAS LIKE living in a permanent state of standing at a crossroads.

He liked being around Clara. Hannah liked being around Clara. And Clara seemed to like being around them. But that was where everything stopped.

They'd been spending more time together. It was easy to be in each other's company. There had been flirting. There had been glances and a bit of innuendo. But he just couldn't seem to take that final step forward. That final...

She was on his mind more or less permanently. But he really didn't want to play this wrong. Yes, they'd shared a kiss in a cupboard. Yes, she'd spent the day with them and several others since. But it was as if he couldn't actually make a move. Ridiculous. If he'd had this conversation with himself he would have scoffed. But taking things further would lead to what, exactly?

Things had been complicated by a call from his sister last night, letting him know that she was pregnant. It had been a complete shock. Georgie had been resolute. No, she wouldn't talk to him about the father. No, she hadn't told their parents yet. Yes, she wanted to have this baby. And yes, she needed some time to think things through.

He'd wanted to get in the car and drive straight up to Scotland. But Georgie must have read his mind because she'd sent him a text five minutes after their call had ended.

I told you because I know how you are about secrets. I kept one from you before and swore I wouldn't do it again. This is my life. You have to let me live it my way. Don't worry. I'll call if I need you. Trust me.

He'd spent most of the night awake, worrying about her. But Georgie knew her own mind. And she'd be a wonderful mother. He knew it, and he had to give her space.

Joshua sighed as he sat down next to Ron, who was typing away on the computer.

'You're making a mess of things,' came the unexpected comment.

Joshua started. He hadn't expected that. 'What do you mean?'

Ron rolled his eyes and lifted his fingers from the keyboard. He turned to face Joshua. 'Clara. You're making a mess of things with Clara.'

Joshua's first reaction was to look around and see if anyone else could overhear their conversation, but the coast was clear. 'I don't understand,' were the words that came out.

Ron's glare was sharp. 'Well, you should. Forgive the expression Joshua, but I'm assuming this isn't your first rodeo?'

Joshua's brow wrinkled. 'What?' Why on earth had he sat here? Was Ron reading his permanently spinning mind?

Ron gaze softened. 'I'm assuming that you've dated a few women in the last few years.'

Joshua gave a slow nod. 'A few,' he said quietly.

'Then why not Clara? We can all see it. You're both like a magnet to metal—you're pulled together. Quite often I'll see the two of you laughing together, or sitting together, and it looks like the next natural reaction would be to put your arm around her shoulders. But you stop yourself. I can see you. You actually start to make the move and then stop.' Ron gave a half-snort. 'Your body and mind and all your senses are telling you to do it. But you don't. Why?'

Joshua wasn't quite sure how he'd been pulled into a conversation like this. 'It's complicated,' he said, stalling for time.

'Actually, it's not,' answered Ron promptly. 'You need to get your act together. I can't tell you if there are stars and rainbows in your future. But, from here, it looks like you don't want to find out. You can't take that risk. Why, Joshua? Clara's a great girl. Do you think there aren't a hundred other guys in this place with her on their radar?'

That made Joshua sit up a little straighter. He hadn't actually thought about that at all.

Ron shook his head. 'Right now, her eyes only seem to look at you. If you don't get your act together, you could miss out on a few months of fun.' He lowered his tone. 'Or you could miss out on the opportunity of a lifetime.' He gave a wry laugh and shook his head. 'And you're the one that's supposed to have the brains between us.'

Joshua was stunned. Ron hadn't said a single word about practically catching them both in the stationery cupboard. Not to him, and apparently not to anyone else. It was unusual in a hospital this size. Usually the first hint of anything sent the rumour mill going, turning the barest whisper of something into a firework display. But for Ron to be so discreet, and yet so direct today? It made Joshua pay attention.

Not that he hadn't been paying attention before...

The phone next to him rang and he picked it up. 'I'll give it some thought,' he murmured to Ron as he walked away, shaking his head at him as if he was the stupidest man to walk the face of the planet.

His pager sounded as he was on the phone to another hospital, giving a second opinion on a really sick child.

Joshua sighed and glanced at the number. A&E. He'd get to it in a minute. But the minute hadn't even passed before the pager sounded again, this time not stopping.

MIA—a major incident alert. It only happened a few times a year. A code red was a paediatric cardiac arrest. Unfortunately, they happened frequently, particularly with the really sick kids in ICU. But MIA was slightly different and always came from A&E. He glanced quickly around the ward and shouted, something he rarely did. 'Ron! Find Isaiah and Clara. Tell them there's a major incident and to assemble in A&E.'

Joshua ran down the stairs of the hospital, meeting several other senior colleagues heading in the same direction. 'What is it this time?' one asked.

He shook his head. 'Don't know yet.'

As they walked through the swinging doors to A&E there was a momentary lull. All the A&E staff were crowded around the nurses' station. Alan Turner was standing on a chair that looked decidedly wobbly.

Alan gave Joshua and a few other Department Heads a nod as they joined the group. 'Okay,' he said, lifting a hand in the air. 'Five minutes ago we got a call about a major Road Traffic Accident, involving up to an estimated seventy casualties. Two buses have collided. One a tour bus, and one a bus with kids on a school trip. A major incident alert has been declared. Our flying squad emergency team have just left to assist on the scene. The Royal Hampstead is the nearest major trauma receiving centre. Twenty ambulances and two air ambulances are on their way to the scene. If you have patients currently in A&E then clear them out. We need all areas. If you have patients upstairs you can discharge, then get some of your colleagues to do it. Beds will be needed.' Alan started pointing at areas and shouting instructions as Clara ran up to join Joshua.

'What is it?' she whispered.

'Major RTA. Up to seventy casualties. A busload of kids is involved.'

She nodded as Alan turned to them. 'Paediatrics will be led by Joshua Woodhouse, Clara Connolly and Isaiah Orun. They'll be based in Resus One and Area Six. Bess, Reid and Fran will assist.'

Joshua spun around and nodded. 'Let's set up,' he said as the nursing staff joined them. They all moved methodically, requesting any specific paed equipment they might need and setting up their own small triage areas for children. Clara and Isaiah moved like the professionals he would have expected. Once they were set up, the silence across A&E was almost deafening. Patients had been moved to X-ray and short-stay areas. Others had been transferred up to ward areas for further assessment. Walking wounded had been sent to a nearby GP practice who helped in emergency situations. And the rest of the staff were just…waiting in an ominous silence.

It was only a few moments before the shrill ring of the red phone at the nurses' station broke the silence. Alan answered quickly, talking in a low voice and taking a few notes. As soon as he replaced the receiver he shouted to his colleagues, 'First set of ambulances are

five minutes out. Eight adults, three paeds—
all major trauma.'

Joshua put his hand on Clara's arm. 'Do
what you can do—and if you need help just
ask. We'll work alongside each other. Hans
is on his way down—he's finishing up in
Theatre—along with a few of the surgeons.
They'll be available to assist.'

He watched her take a deep breath and give
a slow nod. He wondered for a few seconds if
he should worry about her. A major incident
alert wasn't for the faint-hearted. It could be a
time of chaos. Lots of professional staff were
unprepared for what they might encounter and
have to deal with over a short period of time.
But as he watched he saw her give him a serious kind of smile. She was just taking a minute, preparing herself for what lay ahead.

As soon as he'd got the page, Clara and
Isaiah's names were the first he'd thought of.
They were skilled practitioners, and good at
dealing with staff and patients. Clara's straight
to the point attitude was perfect for a situation
like this, and Isaiah's range of clinical skills
would complement the teams.

Joshua glanced around again. Isaiah seemed
to have attached himself to Bess, one of the
most experienced A&E nurses. He was finding himself an anchor for the storm ahead. It

made perfect sense. At a busy time, an experienced A&E nurse was worth their weight in gold. 'Reid, with me please, and Fran with Clara. We'll take resus,' Joshua said, knowing that meant they would have the most badly injured children. But he walked to the main receiving door to stand alongside Alan. If he had a chance to triage all the children first, he would do that.

The first few ambulances appeared in a blaze of sirens and blue lights. Joshua stepped back once he realised the first few patients were adults. Then the children started to appear. The first boy clearly had open fractures. 'Clara, stabilise and get ready for Theatre.' The second boy had multiple facial lacerations. 'Isaiah, assess, stabilise and page plastics.'

The third child was a little girl who was being bagged by one of the paramedics. He met Joshua's gaze. 'Flail chest. Natasha is ten. She was standing in the passageway of the bus and hit the central gear controls.' He rattled off her heartrate, BP and respirations, filling Joshua in on her continued deterioration in the ambulance on the way to the Royal Hampstead.

'Resus One,' he said. 'Any more kids on the way?'

The paramedic shook his head. 'We were the first team. The next will be another ten minutes at least.'

Joshua worked quickly. Flail chests were difficult and quite uncommon in kids. Basically a portion of Natasha's ribcage had separated from the rest of the chest wall. As the paramedic continued to bag her, he could see the uneven way her chest was moving.

One of the other nurses moved to take over the bagging as Reid connected the oxygen supply. Joshua was focused on the little girl, ordering analgesia and sounding her chest while the oxygen support continued. 'Portable chest X-ray,' he ordered. He was certain that at least one of the lungs had been punctured by a rib. He kept his eyes on the oxygen saturation monitor as the X-ray machine was wheeled in.

A face appeared in the doorway—Hans. 'Do you need me?'

'Great,' said Joshua, looking up. 'I was just about to call you. Ventilation may be required. I think there's at least four ribs detached and a strong possibility of a pneumothorax.' He looked down at Natasha again. Even though she was on oxygen her dusky colour was not improving much.

Clara was dealing with her child in the resus

bed next to him. She worked smoothly and competently, ably assisted by Fran. He could see he had no need to worry about her.

A lead apron was passed to him by the radiographer and he slid it over his head, nodding to Reid that he would take over while the X-ray was taking place. Reid waited behind the door alongside Hans, Clara and Fran, for the few seconds it took to take the X-ray.

A few minutes later it was on the viewer next to them. Hans shook his head. Three ribs were obviously misplaced, with one clearly spearing the lung, causing a haemothorax. 'This one needs to be done in Theatre,' he said and Joshua nodded in agreement.

'Absolutely,' Clara agreed as she stepped up alongside him. Her patient was already on his way to Theatre.

Clara reached over and took Natasha's hand, taking a few moments to stand next to the child and talk softly.

Joshua quelled his frustration that he couldn't do something immediately to help this little girl. He'd inserted tubes before to drain the blood from a lung and help reinflate, but not while the rib was still causing damage.

'Consent?' asked Hans.

Joshua looked up once. 'Reid?' was all he said.

A few minutes later the nurse returned,

shaking his head. 'Police say parents have still to be contacted. They can't find Natasha's bag in amongst the wreckage of the bus.'

'No parents?' Concern laced through Clara's voice as she continued to stroke Natasha's hand.

'Darn it. No other responsible adult who could give us the information? Who was Natasha travelling with on the bus?'

Reid shrugged. 'It's bedlam out there. Police just say they're still trying to identify Natasha and get in touch with family.'

Joshua looked down and touched the young girl's arm, for a moment thinking that could be Hannah lying there. Hans was talking with one of the surgeons, making a plan to take Natasha to Theatre.

'Reid? How did the paramedic know her name is Natasha?' Joshua asked.

Reid was washing his hands at the sink. He looked over his shoulder at Joshua. 'Apparently she told the paramedic before she passed out with the pain. But the only info he got was her first name and her age.'

Joshua couldn't imagine this little girl going to Theatre with no one knowing. In an emergency situation like this, they didn't need to gain consent from a parent. Her injuries were potentially life-threatening. He would make a final check with the police that they had no other way to identify Natasha right now and, as Head of Department, would make the call with the surgeon.

He moved around the other side from Clara and took Natasha's hand, bent down and spoke quietly next to her ear. 'Hi, Natasha, I'm Joshua. I'm the doctor that's looking after you. I know you're scared, and I want to promise you we'll look after you. Can you try and give my hand a squeeze?'

He waited for a few moments, sad when nothing happened. He looked up and saw Clara blink back tears. There was no obvious head trauma. Natasha's eyes weren't opening but he checked her pupils again and they reacted as normal to the light he shone in them. She just wasn't showing clear signs of consciousness. When he checked her motor responses, she flinched when he applied a little pain to her fingertip. That was something positive.

He recorded all her responses, then spoke to her again. 'I know that breathing is really tricky right now and we're going to do something to help you with that. You need to go for an operation, but we'll make sure you're sleeping, and when you wake up things should feel a bit easier. We haven't managed to find your family right now, but we'll do our best to sort that out while you're having your operation.' He put his hand gently on her shoulder. 'I'll come back and see you once you've had your operation, but I'm going to let my friend Hans look after you from this point.'

Hans had appeared at his side and checked over the paperwork and electronic charts. As paediatric anaesthetist, he had the final say on whether Natasha would get taken for surgery or not. He gave a nod and took over from Joshua. 'I'll call you when we're out of Theatre.' As he looked around he said, 'I imagine you'll still be here.'

Joshua could hear sirens again as more ambulances pitched up outside. He hated the thought of leaving Natasha with other colleagues, and he could see Clara felt the same way, but he knew they would take good care of her. On a normal day he'd assign a member of his paediatric staff to stay with her, but right now he didn't know how many more paediatric cases they might get, and it was a decision that would have to wait. The surgeon signalled him for a quick chat about agreement on consent for surgery, and Joshua waved to one of their nearby police colleagues for an update on any family. 'We're doing the best we can, but we still have no way of formally identifying Natasha any further right now.'

Joshua nodded and turned to the surgeon. 'In this case we have to treat her under civil law.'

The surgeon also nodded. 'Agreed. If we find parents or relatives later I'm happy to do the explaining with you.'

Joshua waved his hand. 'It's fine. I'm happy to take responsibility.'

The scream of sirens sounded from close by. He looked quickly over to where Clara was reluctantly releasing her hand from Natasha's. For some reason, it seemed entirely natural to be close to her. 'Need anything?' he said quietly.

She lifted her gaze to meet his and gave him a soft, grateful smile in amongst the chaos. 'Just sad that Natasha doesn't have anyone right now. The orthopods have already taken my patient to Theatre.' She snapped on a pair of fresh gloves as Reid helped them wheel Natasha out the resus room. 'I'm ready for the next one.'

She was doing her best to appear cool, calm and collected, even though he'd seen the emotion on her face earlier, and he appreciated that. Something flitted across her eyes. 'What about you?'

He glanced upwards. 'I'm just thanking someone upstairs for coincidences. Hannah is staying at the house of one of her school friends who is having a birthday party tonight. This will be a late one. I'm glad I can stay without panicking about babysitters.'

'I'll stay too,' said Clara quickly. 'You'll need all the help you can get and anyway—' she gave a shrug '—what have I got to go home to if you and Hannah aren't around?'

His heart missed a beat in his chest. She'd said it in a light-hearted tone. But it felt like something more. Like the declaration they'd kind of been heading towards, with both of them tiptoeing around.

He wanted to say so much more, but instead he swallowed and smiled. 'Thank you.'

'No probs.'

'Josh!' The shouting voice made them both turn. 'Four paed cases.'

He moved instantly, triaging quickly and being surprised by a nudge at his elbow. Alice, one of the charge nurses from upstairs, was next to him. He lifted his eyebrows in surprise. 'Executive decision,' she said quickly. 'I've called in extra staff. Lynn's already clearing more space in the assessment unit. You triage and give me all the minors and I'll take them upstairs for assessment. Arun's on the ward and can do his thing.'

He should have known his staff would pull out all the stops in a crisis situation. Lynn was the other charge nurse and Arun one of the other paediatricians. 'I was just about to call you.'

She shrugged. 'You don't need to. We have a shared brain.'

It was true. Staff who had worked together for a long time often anticipated each other's needs. Both Lynn and Alice had been charge nurses in the unit when he'd first arrived. He had a great team and as he noticed Clara giving him a smile as she pulled on a protective gown over her scrubs, ready to receive the next patient, he was reminded how well she was fitting in.

The doors rolled open and an array of patients were brought through. He triaged quickly—one kid unconscious but breathing, another with a crush injury to a leg, one with abdominal wounds. There were another four kids with a variety of bruises, scratches and one little one who was crying. He gave them all a quick check for any hidden injuries. 'Last four mine?' asked Alice as she picked up the weeping four-year-old.

'Perfect,' he said quickly. 'And thank you.'

As Alice dashed off with the other children, Joshua assigned the three more serious kids between himself, Clara and Isaiah. And so the afternoon, and early evening, continued.

He and Clara continued to work side by side in resus. They were a good team, often checking X-rays together or assisting each other when required.

The injuries of the children who arrived became less severe. But all the children who'd been involved in the accident still needed to be assessed to ensure nothing was missed. Several of the parents of the children had also been travelling on the school bus as volunteers, and they had a variety of injuries ranging from minor to severe.

The police did a wonderful job of trying to track and trace the families, considering the tumbling of the bus had meant that nothing had been where it started. A whole host of bags and suitcases had been strewn across the road, some contents unsalvageable.

One of the teachers on the bus had been trapped for a number of hours and had to be cut out, so some of the other school teachers from the same school had come to A&E to help with the children. It turned out that Natasha had been on the tour bus and not, as first presumed, on the school bus. Her grandmother had accompanied her as they were both going on holiday to Spain to meet her mum and dad, but her gran had required surgery for a broken hip. As soon as she'd come round from Theatre she'd started babbling about her daughter, becoming distraught. One of the theatre nurses had immediately recognised the name she kept mentioning and realised the elderly lady was confused from the anaesthetic and managed to join the dots. Both parents were now flying back from Spain. Things were finally starting to fall into place.

By the time Joshua and Clara were finished in A&E they were both tired. 'I need food.' Clara sagged against the nearby wall and wiped her hand across her forehead. She'd needed food about four hours ago but there just hadn't been time.

'Give me five minutes,' said Joshua, the lines around his eyes more pronounced. 'I just need to give Hannah a quick call.'

Clara smiled and followed him into the A&E staff room whilst he grabbed a seat in the corner and pulled out his phone. She poured them both some water from the cooler and sat down beside him. Within a few moments he shook his head, laughing, then spoke for a minute before finishing his call.

'All good?' she asked.

He let out a long slow breath and shook his head and laughed. 'Hannah didn't even want to talk to me. She's having far too much fun. I let the little girl's mum know that I'm likely to spend the night here because of the accident and she can get me on my mobile if she needs me.'

He closed his eyes for a second and rested his head back against the leather chair. It was lumpy, with some ragged tears, but was one of the few chairs in the room that wasn't made out of hard plastic.

She couldn't help herself. She reached over and grabbed his hand. 'Hey, we did good. Things could have been much worse. Everyone who got here got looked after.'

It was true. They'd heard about a few adults on the coaches who had life-threatening injuries. One kid who was seriously injured had been helicoptered to a more specialist hospital, and they'd since heard that the child was serious but stable. But all the kids who had come through the Royal's doors had been assessed and treated as required. Some would have surgical scars, some might need other supports, but all were alive, and as well as could be expected.

He closed his other hand over hers. 'I know,

I know.' He shifted position, leaning forward in the chair so they were closer to each other. 'There was that horrible moment today when I had to send Natasha to Theatre. No one knew who she was; there was no family there for her. And all I could think about was Hannah. And how I would feel if that kid was mine.'

'Of course you did,' said Clara quickly. 'That's what makes you, you.'

Their gazes meshed and a few of the barriers he'd had about this relationship started to melt away. Because he'd seen her face. He knew that Clara had felt exactly the same way that he did. He'd seen her stroke Natasha's hand. He'd seen her talk softly to her. Yes, Clara was here for a short time. But there were so many things about this woman he liked and admired. Right now, he wanted to put his hand at the side of her cheek and pull her in for a kiss. He was tempted to throw caution to the wind, and wonder if he should actually try to give this a go.

He'd kept his heart in a box for the last five years. Losing his wife so quickly and taking over a new role as both parents to their daughter had swamped his time. He'd had a few dates, but was now realising he'd dated, *knowing* he didn't want things to work out.

He'd let lack of trust get in the way. It was

easier never to give himself up to trusting someone else. It was easier to tell himself that he required complete honesty in a relationship before he could even consider moving forward.

It was easier to do that than to admit that allowing himself to trust was allowing himself to put his heart at risk again.

His life was ticking along with only the occasional hiccup—only the occasional doubt that he wasn't doing as well as he could. And this was just it. Every single thought about his personal life always revolved around Hannah. Of course it would—they were a package deal.

But for a few selfish moments he just wanted to think about himself. He wanted to focus on this beautiful woman with the dark brown eyes framed by smudged mascara and tiny freckles across her nose. The one who'd tied her hair up hours and hours ago and not given it another thought since then. She didn't know that her ponytail seemed to have adopted a life of its own and was now in a precarious position at the side of her head.

There was so much about this woman that just drew him in. The way she got straight to the point—she always told him exactly what she thought—but it was clear she had a big heart. He'd seen it in her interactions with kids in the ward, with his daughter and today in A&E.

But right now he wanted to concentrate on the attraction—the way the air between them just seemed to glimmer at times. The look in her eyes that could shoot a bolt of electricity through him. The way she licked her lips. The way she spoke, with her Scottish burr getting more heavily accented the more intense things got between them.

'We need to go back up to the ward,' he said slowly, knowing exactly what he wanted to say next.

'Okay,' she said simply, starting to pull her hand away from his, but he stopped her, tightening his grip around hers.

He lowered his voice to a bare whisper. 'And then we need to talk about the sleeping arrangements, because there is only one on-call room.'

He knew he was looking at her intensely. He couldn't help himself; he still wondered if he was taking the right step.

She leaned forward, her lips brushing against his ear. 'Well, I guess we just need to share then,' she said as she stood up, letting her body brush against his.

It was as if every cell in his body combusted. They were in a room with other staff, even if, because of the emergency situation that had just finished, most of the others were exhausted and no one was paying attention to them. And when Joshua slid his hand back into Clara's as he stood to follow her, no one else seemed to notice. Her footsteps faltered, then she tossed him a glance over her shoulder that set him alight.

Seconds later, as they walked through the door to the stairwell, their lips were on each other. Clara wrapped her hands around his neck, her kisses leaving him breathless. His hands were in her hair, her ponytail band snapping in a ping as their kisses became more intense, making them both laugh.

They stopped for a second and just breathed. 'Let's go upstairs,' she said quickly, pausing to put a hand on his chest before she gave him a wicked smile, 'assess the kids…and then find the on-call room.'

She grabbed his hand and they both ran up the stairs. By the time they reached the ward they were both a little breathless, but had managed to keep their hands to themselves. Both put their professional face into place.

Children had to be reassessed, although, because of the stellar work between Isaiah and Arun, most of them only needed a quick check. Parents were another story. Both Clara and Joshua had to spend considerable time with the parents who had arrived at the hospital with fear in their hearts after hearing their children had been in an accident. Even though other staff had reassured them, Clara and Joshua reassured them again that they would both be around tonight and available if required. The night duty staff had started to appear early, and none of them were surprised to know that two doctors were on call tonight. It wasn't entirely unusual after a major incident, or an outbreak of some sort, that more than one doctor would be available overnight.

When the pizzas that Joshua had ordered arrived on the ward a little later there was enough for everyone, including the kids and parents. Logistics in the ward tonight were awkward. Normally the rules were that each child could have a parent stay overnight if they wished. There were special chairs by each bed that could recline so that they could sleep. But tonight more than one parent wanted to stay, and the ward staff had to juggle and negotiate to find enough space for everyone.

By the time Clara and Joshua headed for the on-call room both were exhausted, but as soon as the door closed behind them it was as if a second wind hit them.

Joshua walked through to the tiny shower

attached to the room and held his hand out to her. 'Shall we?'

She paused for just a second before she very, very slowly started undoing the buttons on her shirt and walked towards him with her hips swinging. 'Why, I thought you'd never ask...'

CHAPTER EIGHT

IT WAS LIKE a whirlwind. One minute she wasn't sure quite what was going on between her and Joshua, and the next she knew *exactly* what was going on between her and Joshua.

They didn't publicise it. But outside work they seemed to merge into one another's lives. Clara was trying to tread carefully, but her heart was powering along like a steam train. Hannah was a normal little girl. She had moments when she clearly wanted her father to herself and Clara could read that and make a graceful exit. There were also times when she seemed to delight in them being together, and others when she would crawl up onto Clara's lap and whisper in her ear, telling her stories about girls at school.

For Clara, the best times were when she could watch Joshua and Hannah together. Their connection was so special. She loved watching them laughing or even quarrelling together. When Hannah tried to cheat him at a board game. Or when she would try and talk him out of a swimming lesson, getting annoyed when he wouldn't concede.

Weeks passed in a blur. Clara had never dated a guy with a child before. She was learning every day. But it seemed that Joshua was adjusting alongside her.

Because of workload responsibilities, plus the fact they were both on call at different times in the week, sometimes they felt like ships passing in the night. As the short-term childcare hadn't really worked out, Joshua had long-standing arrangements with friends who could take care of Hannah overnight when he was on call. He didn't like to ask on any other occasion, meaning that often he and Clara spent time together once Hannah was tucked up in bed.

It was a Friday, and at ten o'clock Clara jumped into the lift with a bottle of chilled rosé in her hands. She was wearing a soft pair of lounge pants and a button-down shirt. She even had slippers on her feet. So when she stepped into Joshua's apartment and saw him dressed in a suit she gave a start.

'Are you going out?'

'No—' he shook his head, smiling, as he took the bottle of wine from her hands

'—we're staying in.' He gestured behind him, where his dining room table was set with a white linen cloth, candles twinkling and red roses in a vase in the centre.

Clara stopped moving, her mouth open in shock. 'What?'

He walked over and pulled out a chair. 'Have a seat. We're having dinner. I'm conscious of the fact I don't really get to take you anywhere grown-up at night because of Hannah. So I thought I would bring the grown-up to us.'

Clara looked down. She was practically wearing pyjamas. 'Hold that thought,' she said as she turned and bolted out of the door. She was a doctor. She had years of practice of yanking on clothes at a moment's notice. Her top was over her head as soon as she walked back through the door, and her lounge pants pulled down as she walked to the bedroom. It took thirty seconds to change her underwear, and another minute to yank a red dress from the cupboard. She pulled it on and slid her bare feet into black patent stilettos. There were still some remnants of today's make-up on her face, so she brushed on some bronzer, re-coated her lashes in mascara and slicked on some red lipstick. She was back out of the door and pressing the button on the lift in less than five minutes.

By the time she got upstairs, Joshua had poured the wine. His eyes widened as she walked with confidence back through the door. She wagged her finger at him. 'Dr Woodhouse, you don't invite a lady to dinner without giving her some notice. Just as well I can dress just as quickly as I can undress.' She winked at him as she sat down in the chair.

'Wow,' was all he said in response, clearly taking in the tighter than normal red dress and extremely high stilettos. Not exactly day-wear. She grinned at the appreciative glance. Ward environments and days out with Hannah didn't exactly let her bring out her sexy side. Now, for the first time since she'd met Joshua, she finally had a chance to bring out what lay beneath the surface. She'd grabbed the first things she could find—which was probably for the best. If she'd known she was coming up for a romantic dinner she would likely have spent all day trying different dresses on. But it appeared her first instincts had paid off.

He couldn't hide the glint in his eye as he handed her a little card. It was inscribed with calligraphy, giving tonight's menu. Her eyebrows raised in surprise. 'This looks as if it came from a starred restaurant.'

He nodded. 'It did. Let's just say I called in a favour that's been offered for a long time. Everything is in the kitchen, ready to be served.'

She licked her lips, taking in his dark grey suit, pale shirt and slim dark tie. He filled it out well. It was much more fitted than any suit she'd seen him wear at work. She wasn't quite sure dinner was what she had in mind.

But, as Joshua disappeared into the kitchen, she crossed her legs and took a sip of her chilled wine. She gave a little giggle as she realised he'd wrapped some white fairy lights around a plant in the corner of the room. That, along with the roses and candles? He'd actually given this some thought.

Her stomach warmed. There was something nice about being planned for. The menu was all food that she loved, and one dish she'd told him that she would like to try. They had been casual conversations, he could easily have forgotten, but it was clear that Joshua either had a great memory or he'd taken notes.

He placed a dome-covered dish in front of her, then lifted the dome with a flourish. She inhaled deeply before looking down at the perfectly formed food in front of her.

Mushroom ravioli in a rich sauce. It was a tiny portion but she knew at a glance what it was, as it was one of her favourites. She pointed to the elaborately shaped napkin sitting on the table. 'I almost don't want to destroy this, but I can't take the chance.'

Before she had a chance to move, Joshua had lifted the napkin and shook out the design, laying it on her lap. She laughed then picked up her knife and fork to try the first course. Every bite was delicious.

'So, tell me how exactly you made this happen?' she asked. Someone had cooked this delicious food and transported it in a manner to keep it at the perfect temperature. She was almost in awe of them for that feat alone.

Joshua sat down opposite her and gave a warm smile. 'I took care of someone's son a few years ago. The little boy had meningitis and had been turned away from the GP surgery twice. His dad brought him to A&E and I realised quickly what was wrong. The little guy was admitted for a few days but recovered. The dad was a starred chef and has constantly been in touch, wanting me to come to his restaurant. This time when he contacted me—' he paused for a second and then gave a half-shrug '—I asked him if there was any possibility the restaurant could come to me.'

'And it did?'

Joshua held out his hands. 'See for yourself. It appears that it does.'

Clara smiled and tilted her head to one side as she looked at her now empty plate. 'That's the thing about these really posh restaurants. They give you tiny portions. It's like they're teasing, and still leaving you wanting more.'

Almost as soon as she said the words she realised her *double entendre* and her cheeks flushed. Joshua started laughing as he picked up her plate, his eyes twinkling. 'Somehow, I think I can relate.'

His skin was tingling with her just being in the room. Something about all this just felt so *right*. And he hadn't been sure that it would. But any lingering doubts were rapidly disappearing.

At first he'd thought Clara might be more comfortable in her relaxed clothes—and there was something nice about the fact that she didn't worry about how she looked before she came up to see him. But her five-minute transformation had been incredible. She had her trademark red lips in place alongside a matching form-fitting dress that just blew him away. When she'd sat down, her shining brown hair around her shoulders, and leaned forward for her glass of wine, giving him a glimpse of her cleavage, he could have spontaneously combusted on the spot. It didn't matter what had come before. Tonight, he'd wanted it to seem like a proper date. He'd wanted it to be special. And it certainly seemed that way.

The more time he spent around Clara, the more the niggling little doubts just seemed to float away, like clouds on a stormy day. Maybe he was just too cautious. Maybe he'd just been truly on his own for too long. Dating and getting close to someone were two entirely different things—and it was only now he was really appreciating it.

What reason could he have not to trust Clara? She'd never given him one. At work, she seemed upfront and honest. Maybe it really was time to shake off his past experience and truly move on.

Clara followed him through to the kitchen, opening the fridge door and taking out the bottle of wine to top up their glasses while he put the plates in the dishwasher. He turned around in time to see her lifting the edge of one of the silver domes and peeking underneath. He moved quickly behind her, slipping his hand around her waist and resting it on her stomach. 'Hey, you'll spoil the surprise. Some might call that cheating.'

She spun around in his arms, winding her hands around his neck. 'I've never been a cheater,' she teased, 'maybe I'm just impatient.' She blinked her dark eyelashes close enough to brush against his cheek. 'Maybe I just want to get to the good part.' She held her breath for a second before moving her lips next to his and whispering, 'Dessert.'

His fingers ran down the length of her spine and she trembled at his touch. 'I'm happy to get to dessert if you are…'

The evening passed too quickly. Clara gathered her clothes and disappeared back down to her own apartment before Hannah woke. But Joshua couldn't sleep. He'd wanted to have a conversation tonight—before they both got distracted. And that conversation, which inevitably hadn't happened, made him nervous. Nervous in both a good and a bad way.

There were only two months left of her job swap. He wanted to ask her what her plans were. He wasn't even sure he'd any right to ask questions like that, but things had heated up between them both so quickly that it felt like the next natural conversation.

Trouble was, this was also a conversation he should have with his sister. Georgie still hadn't told him what her plans were. He was allowed to ask after her pregnancy-related health. But he wasn't allowed to ask anything about the baby's dad. It hadn't taken long to guess it was a fellow doctor from work. Georgie had reassured Joshua that no, the guy wasn't married to, or living with, anyone else. All she said was she wanted to be sure. She seemed to be enjoying the job in Edinburgh. But he had no idea exactly what that meant. Right now, he wasn't sure if she was secretly counting down the days until she returned to London with excitement, with dread, or at all.

A bit like how he wasn't sure how Clara felt.

Part of him wanted her to love working at the Royal and want to stay. A definite part of him hoped that he and Hannah might factor in that equation. But maybe those were unrealistic expectations. She had a permanent job and home in Scotland. It could be that she wasn't thinking quite as favourably on things as he was. It could be he was being entirely selfish. Why should Clara give up her life in Scotland for a life in London, just because that was where *he* lived?

But the thought of uprooting Hannah to a whole new city, a new school, a new circle of friends and activities, made his stomach churn. Would he actually consider doing that to his daughter? Was it even fair?

Joshua let out a sigh and flung off his covers. He wasn't going to sleep at all tonight. He pulled a T-shirt and shorts from his cupboard and strode through to the kitchen to switch on the coffee machine.

But his footsteps faltered as he saw the array of silver domes sitting in the kitchen.

Clara was real. Clara had been here. He could still smell her perfume lingering in the air.

He breathed in deeply. Was he brave enough to take the next step? To have that conversation?

He knew right now he'd be able to tell straight away if he was way off mark. If Clara looked shocked in any way, if she said that she'd never even considered staying, then he'd know. He'd know that he and Hannah didn't feature in her future plans at all. And that would be fine.

Well...of course it wouldn't.

But at least it would be an answer of sorts. It had been a long time since Joshua Woodhouse had opened himself up to the possibility of hurt.

Was he really ready to do that now?

CHAPTER NINE

SHE WAS LIVING the dream. Or at least that was what it felt like.

Every day she spent at least part of her time with Joshua and Hannah. Work was hectic. And she loved that. But the nights she spent on call at the hospital left her with a strange ache in her belly. She missed them. She actually *missed* seeing them.

Last time she'd missed seeing a guy was when she was fifteen and in the first throes of love. That, of course, had lasted around twenty minutes and ended in what felt like a sensationally shattered heart.

This was entirely different.

She'd just finished walking along the Thames before heading back to the flat. The day was gorgeous. The walk had been invigorating. She turned on the coffee machine and walked to open the balcony doors so she could keep bringing a little of the outside in.

She smiled, realising that if she'd been back in Scotland, the outside would probably smell of sheep. Not that she'd ever minded. There were open fields for miles back home, but she was getting used to the view here. She was actually starting to like it.

Clara moved back through to the kitchen, glancing at the calendar as she finished making the coffee. The calendar was beginning to annoy her. The days seemed to pass so quickly. It was bit like a clock, ticking down, stealing time away from her. With a scowl she snatched it off the wall and stuffed it into a nearby drawer. But it wouldn't quite go in there. She frowned, rummaging around to find out what was stopping it sliding inside.

She pulled out a familiar large white envelope. The information from the clinic. The coffee machine made a little noise to indicate it was finished and she pulled out the filled cup automatically, staring down at the contents of the mug and then letting out a wry laugh.

Her coffee normally had a much sweeter taste—her choice was a caramel latte. But Joshua's choice was a double shot cappuccino, and *that* was what she'd made.

She'd done it without thinking, almost on autopilot, and it struck her that part of that made her happy, and part of it made her sad.

She opened the cupboard and took out some sweetener, adding two to the cup, then carrying the coffee and the envelope out to the balcony.

She slid the information from the envelope and looked at it again. It had been weeks since it had arrived. She'd read it over with more than a little interest, but still a lot of uncertainty. It all seemed so...clinical. And that was entirely what it was.

But the end process could be wonderful. She took a sip of the stronger than normal coffee and thought about the time she'd spent with Hannah.

No matter how much she wanted to skirt around it, having a family had always been a dream. She didn't even know if she could carry a child, or if she had viable eggs. This process would find that out.

But the thing that imprinted on her mind most was the experience of having a child in her life. Even when Hannah was in a horrible mood, there was still something deep down in Clara that reminded her it was a privilege to be around a child.

She wanted that, she did. But she didn't have a single clue how to have that conversation with Joshua.

It should be easy: *Hey, Josh—would you ever consider having more kids in the future?*

But she just didn't feel ready to ask that. To presume that she *could* ask that. Maybe he'd decided that losing one long-term partner was enough, and he didn't want to commit fully to someone else again.

It could be he'd decided that he and Hannah were a unit all on their own, with no room for anyone else.

Her stomach twisted. What if she tried to ask the question in a casual kind of way and he gave her that look, as if to say, *You think we might have any kind of future together? Are you crazy?*

The more she thought about it, the more she wondered if this was still a dream to pursue on her own. If she did this on her own, she wouldn't need to worry about anyone else, about what they might think, or if they approved. This was her wish. *Hers.*

Trouble was, she still wanted the dream. The loving partner to share the experience with. A houseful of kids. And meeting Joshua had left her with a whole host of question marks.

She hadn't expected to meet anyone while she was down here. She'd actually wondered if she would *ever* meet someone she'd want to stay with, and that feeling of taking action on her own had been empowering. But did it feel that way now?

Now, she was just confused.

She left the paperwork sitting on top of the envelope on the table and stretched out her legs so they were hiding everything. Her brain tried to tell her she just didn't want the papers blowing away in the gentle breeze, but it was easier to just try and forget about everything right now.

What she really wanted was some more time. Time to think things through. Time to sort out her own head, before sitting down and having the conversation with Joshua.

The phone rang sharply and she jerked, sending the papers scattering onto the tiled floor of the balcony. She made a grab for them as she ducked inside to pick up the phone.

'Clara?' It was Joshua. He sounded harassed.

'What's wrong?' There was no room for preamble.

'The doctor on call tonight has walked off the ward. I need to go in and sort things out. I hate to ask, but Hannah's already in bed. Could you come up to my place?'

Clara was stunned. 'Who's walked off the ward?' It was unimaginable to her. She couldn't understand why any doctor would walk away and leave their patients.

Joshua mentioned the name of another doctor. 'I think he was threatened by some parents over waiting too long for test results. One of them had him up against a wall. Now no one can get hold of him. I have to go in.'

Of course he did. He was the Head of the Department; this was serious.

'I'm on my way,' she said, grabbing a few things before she closed the balcony doors and took her bag and keys.

Joshua was standing at the door with his jacket on when she arrived and he looked at the pile in her hands. She shrugged. 'Pyjamas, clothes for tomorrow in case you need to stay overnight.'

'Thank you.'

She could sense his relief that she was there for Hannah. She gave his shoulder a squeeze and brushed a brief kiss on his lips. 'Absolutely no problem. Call me later.'

He nodded and disappeared out of the door.

It was weird being in Joshua's place without him. But Clara dumped her stuff and went to check on Hannah first. Despite what her father had said, Hannah was clearly not sleeping. She'd bundled her bedcovers up and had a variety of dolls and cars playing across mountains and valleys.

Her eyes widened when Clara raised her eyebrows at her from the door. 'Clara! What are you doing here?'

She ran over and gave Clara a huge hug. Clara melted a little, just like she always did around Hannah. She patted the bed to get her to sit back down. 'There's an emergency at the hospital and your dad's had to go and deal with it. So I'm here until he comes back, or maybe for the whole night.' She could see Hannah's school clothes, shoes and bag already laid out for tomorrow. At least there wouldn't be a scramble to find everything.

'Ooh!' There was an immediate gleam of mischief in Hannah's eyes. 'What can we do?'

But Clara was too wise for a bit of manipulation. '*We*,' she said quickly, 'can check the time and see that someone I know should actually be sleeping right now. Let's get these toys away.' She started picking up the dolls and cars. 'Why don't you pick a book and I'll read that to you before you go to sleep.'

Disappointment swamped Hannah's face. 'Okay, pick two then,' said Clara quickly. 'But you have to get to sleep. You've got school in the morning.'

Hannah slouched over to her white bookcase and took a few moments to pick two. Moments later she was back in bed with both books in her lap.

Clara settled onto the bed beside her and looked at the books. She didn't recognise either of them.

'Okay, let's start with this one.'

She wrapped an arm around Hannah's shoulders, letting her snuggle in and holding the picture book in front of them both. She was delighted to find it was a story about a little girl who wanted to be an astronaut and decided to make herself a suit out of things she found around the house. The story was comical and the illustrations perfect and they chatted throughout.

'Is this one of your favourites?'

Hannah nodded. 'I want to be an astronaut,' she said with the determination of a five-year-old.

'You want to go into space?'

Hannah nodded enthusiastically.

'Why space? Why don't you want to be a deep sea diver? Or an Arctic explorer? Or a pirate?' She pulled random ideas from nowhere as they snuggled together. There was something so nice about just having a little time together.

Hannah turned her big eyes towards her.

'I want to go to space to see if I can catch Mummy. She's one of the stars up there.'

Clara's stomach clenched instantly, but her heart expanded in her chest.

Out of the mouths of babes…

She'd heard the expression many times but never felt a punch in the gut like now. The range of emotions was overwhelming, and she knew she had to handle this carefully.

'Who told you about Mummy being a star?'

'Daddy and Auntie Georgie. There's a star up in the sky that has Mummy's name. I sometimes look for it at night. But I'm not always sure what one it is.'

She stopped for a second then wrinkled her little brow. 'They told me they gave the star Mummy's name when I was little. Just a baby.'

Clara nodded, trying to choose her words carefully. But she didn't get a chance. Hannah seemed to want to keep talking. 'I don't really remember her,' she said in a small voice, tinged with guilt.

Clara let her hand push some of Hannah's bed-ruffled hair back from her face. 'Oh, honey. That's okay. You were tiny. No one expects you to remember. I don't know anyone who can remember things from when they were a baby.'

She noticed the photo frame across the

room; Hannah was staring at it. Even from here, Clara could see the pale-faced woman with brown hair and the baby bundle in her arms. Clara's heart gave a twist as she thought about what Abby had sacrificed to make sure her daughter got into this world safely. But the overwhelming feeling she got when she looked at that photo was love. It was clearly written across Abby's face. She knew she wasn't going to see her daughter grow up. She knew she didn't have much time left. And the photo captured the joy and love in her face for her daughter.

'People tell me stories,' said Hannah slowly.

Clara drew her eyes away from the picture. 'What kind of stories?'

'Dad…' Hannah looked down at her hands '…and sometimes Auntie Georgie. They tell me things about Mummy. Things they all did together. And Daddy says he's got things to show me when I'm older.' Her fingers twisted the blanket on her lap as she shook her little head. 'But I don't remember things—' her voice broke a little '—and I think they want me to.'

A lump formed in Clara's throat immediately and she pulled Hannah up into her lap. The little girl's confusion was palpable. And

Clara couldn't help but wonder how long she'd held this inside.

She smoothed down Hannah's hair with one hand as she spoke. 'Hannah, your daddy and your auntie know that you don't remember your mummy. They wish that you did, and that's why they tell you stories. They want you to know things about her. Like how much she loved you, how much fun she was, and how important you were to her.'

Hannah blinked and bit her bottom lip.

Clara felt as if her heart might break for her. She cupped Hannah's face in her hands. 'It's okay, honey. It's okay not to remember. As you get bigger you might want to find out some things about your mummy, and that's when you can ask any questions you like, and your dad, and your auntie, will be able to answer them for you. But this isn't something to worry about. Not at all. The important thing to remember is that you are a very special girl and that you're loved, by lots of people.'

She pulled Hannah into a hug as her own eyes brimmed with tears. Hannah wrapped her arms tight around Clara's neck. After a little while she whispered, 'Clara?'

'Yes?'

'Will you keep cuddling me until I fall asleep?'

'Of course I will.' Clara moved on the bed, letting Hannah lie down next to her and wrapping her arm around her when she moved to cuddle in close.

Her heart was full of love for this little girl, and her heart was also full of love for Joshua. She'd thought the most difficult conversation she'd have with Joshua was about their potential future together. Now, she wondered if the most difficult conversation she'd have would be about Hannah. Was there any way to talk about this delicately?

He was Hannah's father. He deserved to know that his daughter was struggling a little—and that he, however unwittingly, and with the best will in the world, might be contributing to it.

She squeezed her eyes closed for a second as dread swept over her. She'd have to time it carefully. She didn't want to say anything to upset him. But the truth was, if she cared about him she had to let him know. No matter how hard it was.

Her free hand moved back and forth, doing soft strokes across Hannah's hair as she willed her to sleep.

Was this what being a parent was like? Knowing you had to do what was right first?

Through in the other room she could hear

her mobile ring. It would be Joshua, telling her how things had worked out at the hospital. She wanted to answer, she really did. But if she moved she might disturb Hannah.

So she let the phone ring, and kept holding onto Hannah tightly.

There would be time to talk later.

She just had to work out when.

CHAPTER TEN

JOSHUA PICKED UP the mail and stared down at the envelope in his hand. It was cream, good quality but looked a bit battered. The name on the front was definitely his—Dr Joshua Woodhouse—but the calligraphy on the front had obviously been written with a fountain pen and had been smeared at some point on the journey, meaning the end of the street address was almost illegible. Someone had scored through the smearing and written an alternative address—*24F Park Road?*—with a red pen, and that had been followed by *Not at this Address*. Another hand had written *24F Park Tower?*, which was where the envelope had finally ended up.

As he tore open the envelope he was amused by the travels of whatever was inside. A cream card with a tell-tale picture on the front fell into his hand. His stomach clenched. From the sketch of a bride and groom on the front it had to be a wedding invitation.

He flipped it open, scanning the words.

Alyssa Hart and David Jenner
would like to invite
Dr Joshua Woodhouse and partner
to celebrate their marriage on...

He let out a groan. Of course. Both Alyssa and David had been on his university medicine course. He knew they were getting married—they might even have sent one of those 'save the date' cards but he'd completely forgotten. In all honesty, he hadn't been invited to many weddings over the last few years. He was sure most of his friends thought of him as the awkward single guest—plus they knew he was a lone parent to Hannah. But Alyssa and David had insisted he come to the wedding. The date made his stomach flip. This weekend. Just how long had this invitation been bouncing around?

He examined the envelope. Sure enough, the postage date was six weeks before. And, since they'd already sent him a save the date, he was sure he wouldn't get out of it with the usual *Sorry, I'm scheduled to work* that he had pulled before when he'd been invited to social events.

His thoughts started spinning. His parents had already offered to come and take Hannah away for that weekend to their caravan just outside Brighton. He had planned to surprise Clara in some way. He'd even toyed with the idea of taking the train to Paris and staying overnight somewhere. But he hadn't booked anything—and now it looked like he had a wedding to attend.

He leaned against the wall for a few moments. Of course, the only person he would invite would be Clara. But would she actually want to go? The wedding would be full of people who'd known him years ago. Some of them might actually have attended his own wedding, and he knew that Clara would get a few curious glances. He paused—was it fair to ask her? It wasn't that his friends would say anything awkward or inappropriate… Then again, it was a wedding, alcohol would be involved, and his friends might say something *entirely* awkward or inappropriate.

But he wanted to get back out there. He *wanted* to introduce Clara to his friends. He didn't want to continue to be the sad, lonely, widowed single friend. Clara was gorgeous.

She was funny and smart and he wanted his friends to know that he'd met someone who...

His brain stopped dead. He'd met someone who...? Who he hadn't managed to have the *What do you think about us and the future?* conversation with yet. He looked down at the invite again. RSVP by... Oops. The date had long since passed.

He picked up his phone and sent a text message to David, who replied a few minutes later.

About bloody time. Alyssa's having a nervous breakdown at the amount of people who haven't RSVP'd. You've just got yourself off the hit list by the skin of your teeth. Can't wait to see you!

He smiled. The last few days had been a bit odd between him and Clara. It was as if she was always waiting to say something, but just couldn't get there. The pessimistic part of him wondered if it might be telling him they needed to cool things down as she'd be leaving soon. But the optimist in him hoped she might say she wanted to stay.

Maybe this invite would give her the push either way. It would be the first formal event they'd attend as a couple. Joshua glanced down at the venue. A beautiful hotel towards Essex set in large grounds. The invite included a number for guests to call to book a room to stay overnight if they wished. He dialled it immediately, hoping because he'd left it so late they wouldn't be assigned the broom cupboard under the stairs.

By the time he'd replaced the phone, plans had fallen into place in his head. He'd invite Clara to this wedding—he knew she was free this weekend. If she accepted, then he'd use the opportunity to have the conversation with her that had been stalling these past few weeks. It was time. He felt good about it. He wanted to be honest with her. He wanted to be able to consider a future with her, and with Hannah.

He couldn't ignore the fact that she was always the first person he wanted to talk to—the first person he wanted to see. He couldn't pretend that his heart didn't skip a couple of beats like a crazy teenager when he saw her laugh, or he noticed the wicked twinkle in her eyes.

After a few years in hiding, his heart felt ready to take the next step. To trust someone again. To try and make a go of this relationship and take pleasure in imagining where it might go. Maybe things wouldn't work out, but he was certain he wanted to try. And the only person he wanted to try with was Clara.

* * *

It had been an odd kind of day. The wedding
had been sprung on her. When Joshua had told
her Hannah was spending the weekend with
her grandparents she'd hoped they would do
something together. A wedding was a little
unexpected, and she couldn't pretend that she
wasn't a bit nervous. Nervous enough to take
herself off to some exclusive boutique recommended by a particularly stylish fellow doctor and try on the contents of the whole shop.

An hour earlier she'd met Joshua's parents
as they'd waved Hannah off. If his parents had
been surprised to see her they hadn't shown it
for a second. Linda and Alastair were warm
and welcoming, both giving her hugs and appearing genuinely happy to meet her. But,
more importantly, it was clear they absolutely
doted on their granddaughter. It was equally
clear that Hannah had them both wrapped
around her little finger. It was interesting to
see Joshua interact with his parents. It was obvious they were immensely proud of both of
their children, and the resemblance between
Joshua and his father had been obvious. They
both had tall slim frames and a similar gait.
But his mannerisms mirrored his mother's,
from the way he sometimes talked with his
hands to the way he inclined his head a lit-

tle while listening to someone, and that made Clara smile in amusement.

By the time they'd waved Hannah off, Clara only had forty minutes to get ready before they had to leave to drive to the wedding.

She'd thrown some things into an overnight bag but, because no one could ever predict what the traffic would be like in London, she'd decided just to wear her outfit for the wedding.

It took ten minutes to put her make-up on and get ready. She carried her fascinator in the cute little box it had been packaged in, rather than perch it on her head for the journey. She was just spraying some perfume and touching up her lipstick when Joshua came into the apartment. 'Knock, knock,' came the deep voice. 'Want me to grab your bag?'

'It's by the door,' she said as she stuffed her lipstick into her matching clutch bag.

The women in the shop had been very entertaining. They'd played music and brought out champagne while she'd tried on dresses. With each dress they'd managed to magic matching shoes, jewellery and fascinators to try on. But they hadn't been overbearing. 'Oh, no!' one of them had exclaimed as she'd stepped out in a silver sequin design. 'That colour wipes you out.'

The design of a tomato-red dress had been

vetoed too. And it had actually felt like shopping with friends. Now she understood why her colleague had recommended this place. They gave her confidence that, whatever she left with, she wasn't going to look like some kind of fool who'd been duped into buying something unsuitable.

It wasn't her normal kind of thing. But she hadn't wanted it to be. This weekend already felt special. She couldn't pretend she didn't want to make a good impression with Joshua's friends.

She took a deep breath and stepped out the bathroom. 'How do I look?'

He was bending over, picking up her carry-on-size suitcase, and he glanced over his shoulder and promptly dropped the suitcase on his foot.

He straightened, giving her a good view of his dark navy suit, white shirt and pink tie. She'd handed it to him last night with a wink. 'Just making sure we'll match.'

From the expression on his face, the larger than usual balance she'd paid had been money well spent.

'You look stunning,' he said simply as he stepped forward, shaking his head a little. He held out one hand. 'Am I allowed to touch as long as I don't spoil anything?'

She glanced down. Her mid-pink sleeve-less silk dress was the sleekest item she'd ever owned. From the deep cowl neck, it clung to every curve, skimming her hips and falling straight to the floor. Only the three-inch heels kept it from touching the ground.

'What's the point of looking but not touching?' she teased.

His hands grasped her firmly as he took her by surprise and bent her backwards as he kissed her. She laughed, grabbing a hold of his shoulders. 'Aren't we supposed to save this for the dance floor later?' she said breathily.

'I couldn't wait that long,' he said as he trailed kisses down the side of her throat.

'You'll make us late for the wedding,' she giggled.

He sighed and tilted her upwards again. 'Spoilsport.'

She shrugged and dusted imaginary dust from his shoulders. 'You don't scrub up too badly yourself.'

He held her for a few more seconds and she could see something flitting across his eyes. Her heart missed a couple of beats. But then he leaned forward and spoke quietly into her ear. 'Let's just have fun this weekend. Deal?'

Relief flooded through her. For half a second then she'd been worried. But then, she'd been thinking herself about the conversations they needed to have and wondering when it would be appropriate. The thought of forgetting about all that and just having fun sounded like heaven.

'Deal,' she agreed as she dropped a kiss on his cheek, leaving a hint of lipstick there. She could have lifted her fingers to smudge it away, but she liked it. That almost invisible mark on his cheek. A sign that he was hers.

They made it to the Essex wedding venue with ten minutes to spare, thanks to the diversions and hideous London traffic. Any plans he might have had to sit for a while, enjoying a glass of wine before the wedding were well and truly blown.

By the time they'd put their bags in the room and Clara had put some magnificent creation on her head they were almost out of time.

'Wait,' he said as she put her hand on the door.

'What is it? Have I got lipstick on my teeth?' She squinted over at the mirror.

He laughed. 'No. I arranged to get something delivered.' He glanced around the room, spying a cardboard box in a cool spot. He walked over and lifted the lid, smiling when he saw what was inside.

Clara appeared at his shoulder. 'What's in there?' She gave a little gasp and he could swear he could hear the smile in her voice. 'You bought me a corsage?'

She sounded kind of stunned. 'Of course I bought you a corsage.' He lifted the delicate ringlet of flowers for her wrist. 'After you gave me the tie last night, I phoned the hotel to see if they could arrange a buttonhole for me, and a corsage for you in the colour you'd specified.'

He held up the tiny roses that exactly matched her dress, encased in some greenery and entwined around a pearl corsage for her wrist.

'It's beautiful,' Clara sighed. She twisted her wrist one way and then the other, admiring it, before reaching in and taking out his matching buttonhole. His was a single large rose in exactly the same shade of pink. 'Let me.' She smiled as she fastened it onto his suit.

'We're a matching pair,' he said quietly, catching sight of them both in the mirror. His heart squeezed in his chest. This was it. This was what he wanted. A partnership.

Her hand came up to his chest as she turned to see where he was looking.

It was like a moment in time. To the outside world they looked like the perfect couple.

Her in her slim, sleek pink dress with shining hair, sparkling eyes and leaning into him. He, in turn, in his smart suit, matching buttonhole, with his arms wrapped around her waist. Both smiling.

People could look. Mention how matched they were. Both paediatricians. Both hard workers.

He didn't have a badge above his head saying single parent and widower. She didn't have a badge above her head saying that she was only here on a temporary basis.

His overwhelming urge was to make this permanent. To make the move, have the conversation and put his heart on the line once more. To take a chance on trusting someone again.

Clara's reflection smiled at him, then her face turned up towards his. 'Are you okay?'

She must have seen something in his eyes. He dropped a kiss on her lips and didn't hide the fact that he inhaled deeply, taking in what he now knew was her signature scent. The smell of summer flowers in the rain.

There was still something burning deep inside him. Doubt. Something he couldn't put his finger on and he hated that. He knew how he felt. He knew what he wanted to do. But, for all that Clara didn't seem to have any reason not to feel the same way, he still felt as if there was something he didn't know. Something she hadn't shared.

It was odd and had never been entirely obvious. Of course, he didn't think there was a hidden relationship anywhere, or something traumatic in her past that she hadn't shared. But there was just something—something else.

He stared down into those deep brown eyes. For right now, he could see nothing. All he could feel was the potential for this weekend. He pushed his doubts aside and smiled, putting his hand into hers.

'Let's go have some fun.'

The wedding was perfect in every way. They hurried down the stairs into the large, beautiful sunny room set out for the ceremony and slid into some seats next to people who were clearly friends of Joshua's. He leaned forward and whispered to them, 'Ben, Roma, this is Clara.'

Both smiled and stretched their hands to shake with Clara while she tried not to puzzle over the introduction. Clara. Clara who? His workmate? His girlfriend? His casual friend?

She didn't get much of a chance to think about it. 'Gorgeous dress,' Roma whispered to her as the music started and the groom and his best man walked down the aisle, shaking hands with friends.

The ceremony was beautiful and the bride wore a lace-covered cream gown and carried a bunch of yellow flowers. Joshua had told her that these were two of his oldest friends—he'd trained with them, which meant that they must have known Abby. She couldn't pretend that didn't make her nervous. But didn't the fact he'd brought her here in the first place to meet them mean something?

After the ceremony the guests mingled in the grounds next to the outside bar while the wedding party had their photographs taken. Everything seemed very informal. As Clara was standing at the bar, getting her glass of white wine topped up, she felt a nudge at her elbow. She was shocked when she turned around and found herself enveloped in a hug from the bride.

'You must be Clara,' she said as her veil brushed against Clara's cheek. 'I'm Alyssa. I'm so happy to meet you.' She signalled to the bartender, who gave her a glass of champagne.

'Nice to meet you too,' said Clara quickly, a little stunned. She wasn't too sure that Joshua had specified to the bride and groom who he was bringing with him. 'Your dress is absolutely gorgeous.'

'Thanks. So is yours. That colour really suits you. So, you're working with Joshua and staying in Georgie's flat?'

Clara barely had time to nod before Alyssa continued. 'What do you think of Hannah? Isn't she adorable?'

Clara started to relax a little. Maybe it was the second glass of wine. She answered completely truthfully. 'Hannah is great. I love being around her.'

Alyssa tilted her head. 'I love your accent.'

A voice started calling Alyssa's name in the distance but she waved her hand. 'Oh, they can wait. I want to know more about you. Can we catch up later after dinner? David and I both really want to get to know you.'

It was ridiculous but the hairs on Clara's arms gave an uncomfortable prickle. Why was she nervous? Of course Joshua's friends might be curious about her, but this seemed like a bit of a test—what if she didn't pass?

'You're the bride.' She smiled. 'You're the boss. I'd love to meet your husband too at some point. Joshua told me you all trained together.'

Alyssa nodded and gave a sad smile. 'A long time ago. We're all getting old now.' She gestured across the garden. 'It's taken ten years for David and me to finally organise getting married.' She looked back at her, and Clara could see it in her eyes. The unspoken words. The words about Abby.

She decided to address the elephant in the room. 'You must have gone to Joshua and Abby's wedding then?'

It was easier just to have it out there. She didn't want Alyssa to feel awkward about mentioning someone who'd presumably been a friend.

Alyssa nodded and put her hand on Clara's arm. 'We're so glad he's brought you. I wasn't sure that he'd bring anyone. I mean, he's dated, but it's never been serious. He's always been so focused on Hannah that I wasn't sure he would ever find room in his life for another person.'

Clara took a gulp of her wine. It wasn't such a strange thing to say. But it still made her feel self-conscious. Alyssa finished her champagne and gave her a smile. 'We'll chat after dinner. I'll bring David over to meet you.'

Clara gave her a smile of relief. 'Can't wait, and again, you look beautiful.'

Alyssa waved her hand and drifted off in a froth of cream lace as Clara let out a big breath. Joshua was crossing the grass towards her from where he'd been in a conversation with someone else. Alyssa met him on the way and he spun her around, laughing, before she whispered something in his ear while winking back at Clara.

But Joshua's eyes stayed fixed on Clara. And as he walked towards her with a big grin on his face she felt as if she was the only woman there.

He slid his hands around her waist and bent to kiss her. If she had any doubts about what role she had here they all vanished in an instant. 'Having fun yet?' he whispered.

The nervous flicker in her stomach dissipated at his touch. 'I'm with you,' she said softly. 'Of course I'm having fun.'

She started to relax a little. Joshua took her over and they sat in the garden with the couple who'd they sat next to at the ceremony. Ben and Roma were old work colleagues of Joshua's too. Ben was a radiographer and Roma a fellow doctor. They laughed and joked easily, telling her tales of work disasters. Several other guests came and joined them from time to time, all welcoming Clara warmly.

The weather was warm and when they were invited back inside for dinner the glass doors that led to the gardens were left open to allow the air to circulate. Dinner was served quickly and the food was delicious. They were seated at a table with some of the groom's relatives, as well as some of Joshua's friends. Chat was light, and by the time the evening reception was due to start Clara was beginning to wonder if this was turning into the perfect day.

As they watched the first dance Joshua's arm was tightly around her waist. 'Hey,' he said huskily in her ear, 'I've never asked you. Do you like to dance?'

'Would you like to find out?' She leaned back against him and he made a low noise.

His lips touched the back of her neck. 'You have no idea.'

As the music started for another tune she took that as a yes and stepped out onto the dance floor, beckoning him with one finger.

One of his friends let out a wolf whistle as Joshua took his cue and followed her. He took her firmly in his arms and swept her around the floor, his footsteps sure and confident. She was surprised at just how good he was. 'Hey, ballroom dancer,' she joked. 'Got any other secrets you want to share with me?'

'What can I say? My sister told me as a teenager I had to find some kind of rhythm and dance. Girls like to dance. So I learned.'

Clara grinned. 'Ah, so this was just some kind of technique to get girls?'

'Absolutely.' He nodded. Then he glanced over his shoulder in some kind of mock act. 'Is it working?'

'We'll see,' Clara teased as she kept spinning around him.

They danced until her feet hurt in her high shoes. She took them off and put on a pair of flip-flops that had been supplied for the women. Evening snacks appeared, cupcakes with *Mr and Mrs* on them, traditional wedding cake, rolls with bacon, rolls with sausage, alongside bowls filled with tomato sauce and brown sauce. Joshua started laughing. 'This,' he said, lifting up one of the rolls, 'this is how Alyssa and David met. David came in late to halls one night. Alyssa had just made herself a bacon roll and ducked back to her room to grab her sauce. By the time she came back, David was eating it.'

'What?' Clara started to laugh, then wrinkled her nose. 'She kept her sauce in her room?'

Joshua nodded solemnly. 'Of course, it was hide or die in those halls. Anything you put in the cupboards in the kitchen disappeared. Literally, in an instant. We all thought some kind of hungry ghost lived there.'

'But, in this case, the ghost was David?'

Joshua nodded. 'He'd gone on ahead when

we'd left the pub. By the time I got in, Alyssa was hitting him over the head with a cushion. He offered to give the roll back, but he'd put brown sauce on it, and she hated it.'

'Where did he get brown sauce in the middle of the night if he hadn't gone back to his room?'

'Aha,' said Joshua slowly. 'We—I and a few of my fellow students—had a hiding place for essentials in one of the vents. We would never have left cooked bacon unguarded. As soon as you started cooking food in the kitchen people would appear from nowhere. It was definitely survival of the fittest.'

He pulled her down onto his knee, one hand resting on her leg. 'You've been great today. I know it might have been hard—mixing with my friends and a whole bunch of people you didn't know. But…' he reached up and touched her cheek '…thank you. I appreciate it.' He looked out across the crowded room. 'It's been a long time since I've come to something like this and actually enjoyed myself.'

She breathed in slowly, taking a minute to say the right thing. 'Why?' she asked simply.

His eyes connected with hers. 'Because I hadn't found the right person to come with.' The words made her heart melt. He couldn't have said anything more perfect. She picked up a cupcake and held out her hand to him. 'How about we take some of these things back as room service?'

He stood up and crossed over to the bar, coming back a few seconds later with a bottle of champagne and two champagne flutes. Clara had a little pile of cupcakes on the plate. 'Ready?' she asked.

'Always.' Her heart skipped a few beats as they made their way back to their room.

The service had turned down the bed, put some chocolates on the pillows and left the curtains open, showing a beautiful view of the gardens. At this time of night the gardens were lit by multicoloured lights that glowed on and off, giving the impression of a magical wonderland. Joshua put down the champagne on the table at the window and turned to take Clara in his arms.

'How did you find it today?' She could hear the tinge of anxiety in his voice.

'I've had a great time,' she reassured him. 'Your friends have all been lovely.'

He swallowed and paused for a second. 'A few of them asked me.'

'Asked you what?'

'Asked me if we were serious.'

She felt herself stiffen. Now it was her turn to swallow. 'What did you say?'

In the dim lights his eyes fixed on hers. 'I told them I'd like to be, but wasn't sure what you wanted.'

Her breathing stuttered and skin prickled. The question. The conversation she'd been waiting for. 'What about Scotland?' she breathed.

His gaze lowered. 'That's up to you. I could never ask you to give up a home or job that you loved.'

Something plucked at her heartstrings. She remembered the first time she'd walked into Georgie's flat and thought it resembled a show house instead of a home. Her place was much more low-key. Much more cosy.

Her voice trembled. 'How do you feel about long-distance relationships?'

He tilted his head to one side—a movement that reminded Clara of his mother. 'I think,' he said steadily, 'that it might be worth a try.' A little flare of hope fired inside her belly. He was actually considering it.

'London and Edinburgh aren't that far apart. Four hours by train.'

He must have been checking. More hope.

'And we could talk every day and video chat to catch up.'

His hand slid over the smooth silk of her dress. 'But it's not quite the same, is it?'

Her mouth dried. She knew exactly what he was saying. It wasn't the same. It wasn't the same as being able to climb a few flights of stairs and walk into his flat on a nightly basis. It wasn't the same as seeing him every day at work. How would she feel with some distance between them?

She knew instantly that she didn't want that. 'It's not the same,' she whispered. 'I can't imagine not seeing you or Hannah on a daily basis.'

Her heart was sinking. Hannah was settled at school and Joshua was in charge of a department at one of the best hospitals in London. Any decision to be made had to be hers.

Part of her wished she'd tried to phone Ryan before tonight—to talk things through with him. To see what he would think if she told him she might not want to come back to Scotland at all. Would he be surprised? Angry? Or pleased for her?

Joshua reached up and stroked her cheek. 'I can't imagine not seeing you every day either.' He let out a low laugh and shook his head. 'I've been so worried about having this conversation with you.'

'You have?'

He nodded. 'We haven't had a conversation about the future. I wasn't even sure how you would react if I asked you about it. I was worried I had read this all wrong.'

She pressed her lips together and nodded too, laying her hand on his chest. 'I've been worried too. Worried that you might think I was trying to insert myself into your lives—into a place I might not be wanted.'

'Oh, you're wanted,' he said in a deep voice. 'You have no idea how much you're wanted.'

She moved her hands to his shoulders, trying to take her attention away from the fact that Joshua had started moving his fingers oh-so-lightly down her spine.

'What about Hannah? What do we tell Hannah?' She knew there was another part of this conversation, but it just didn't feel like the right moment.

'We tell Hannah the truth,' he said firmly. 'We tell her that we're dating and, because your job was only agreed for a short time, we're trying to find a way to make it work.'

Clara was still a little nervous. 'How do you think she'll react?'

He took a little time to answer. 'You've seen her happy, you've seen her having a temper tantrum.' Her stomach flipped because she'd seen other things with Hannah that she'd need to talk to him about. He gave her a smile that was half proud, half sad. 'I have nothing else to compare her to, but I'm sure she's in every way a normal five-year-old.' He took a deep breath. 'But I think she's ready, Clara. I think she's ready to have someone else in her life—' he pulled her closer '—just like I am.' He murmured the words against the skin of her cheek. 'We love you, Clara. We want you in our lives.'

Her heart swelled in her chest. These were just the words she wanted to hear. The reassurance. The commitment. The perfect final piece of the jigsaw puzzle slotting into place.

She answered from the bottom of her heart. 'That's what I want too.'

His fingers continued their sensuous dance down her spine and she let out a little giggle. 'What are you doing to me, Joshua? You're going to drive me crazy.'

He dipped her backwards. 'Exactly my plan.' His grip was firm, making her feel safe and secure.

'I like your plans. And I liked you dancing. You know, letting loose a little. How about some more?'

He pulled her upwards and slid out his phone, filling the room with slow, sensual music. Perfect. She merged her body against his, their curves melding together, as if they were made to be this way.

As they moved in gentle steps, Joshua

trailed kisses down her neck. She'd hoped this would be a special weekend. Now she knew the man who had stolen her heart felt the same way she did. Everything seemed to be aligning. Even though she'd need to sort out logistics about her house and her job, it all felt worth it.

Worth it to feel like this for a lifetime.

CHAPTER ELEVEN

THE NEXT FEW weeks kind of floated by. Clara looked online at other suitable job vacancies in London. The job swap had been unique. Most positions at her level were recruited for more than a year in advance and, unless someone pulled out at short notice, there might not be a vacancy.

She toyed with the idea of connecting with Georgie. She had no idea how things had worked out with her placement at the hospital in Edinburgh. Was there even a remote possibility that Georgie might like to continue there?

It seemed too ridiculous, so Clara put it out of her mind.

Joshua was charming at work, easy to be around, and most of the other members of staff had guessed that something was going on between them. Ron had given her a few raised eyebrows, then told her that he was delighted for them both.

She couldn't stop smiling. And she couldn't remember the last time she'd felt like that. Things were going so well she was considering coming off the meds she'd started taking months ago. She didn't want to do it without talking to her GP first, but getting an appointment was proving tricky.

The countdown on the calendar was feeling ominous, the end of the swap creeping closer and closer. Soon, it would be time to pack up her belongings and drive the long road back up to Scotland. She should feel happy to see some of her old colleagues, her best friend Ryan—who she'd badly neglected since she'd been down here—and to see the views from her old cottage again with all the fields and sheep.

But, even though she knew she should be happy, there was still a feeling in the pit of her stomach. Or two actually. One, because she wasn't looking forward to going home the way that she should—and that made her feel a bit guilty. And two, because she still had something really important to do first.

Hannah. She had to have the conversation with Joshua about Hannah. She'd tried a few times, but it had never seemed quite the right moment. But it was beginning to feel that there would never be the right time to have this kind of difficult conversation. She had a duty. To herself, to Hannah and to Joshua.

If there was any chance of them being a family together, she had to prepare herself for times like this. She was still a bit of an outsider—but that might have been why Hannah had confided in her.

As a doctor, keeping confidences was always an issue. Times at work could be tough, and child and family protection issues meant that confidences had sometimes to be broken in order to protect those who needed it.

Of course those kind of issues didn't apply to Hannah but, as a compassionate adult, Clara knew she had to let Joshua know how his little girl was feeling. His wife, Abby, was such a sensitive subject. She had been mentioned in passing, more so since they'd been at the wedding together and Clara had met a number of their mutual friends. None of those people had made her feel uncomfortable. Clara wasn't that type. She didn't expect people who'd known Abby to feel as if they couldn't mention her in Clara's presence.

Joshua had loved and respected his wife. That much was clear. But he was ready to move on. He'd told her that, and she believed him. She didn't have the feeling that she was taking someone's place, or living in their shadow, and that gave her the security in this relationship that she needed.

But it still didn't excuse her for not being brave—for not bringing up the subject before now.

Clara sighed and stretched as she looked out of the window. She'd emptied a few drawers in the kitchen, trying to sort out what she needed to keep and what she needed to get rid of. When she'd arrived here, Georgie had this place as neat as a show home and whilst Clara wasn't quite up to those standards, she wanted to make sure things were still kept tidy.

The door clicked and Joshua walked in, a broad smile on his face. He flung his backpack into a corner and wrapped his arms around her, shuffling her backwards towards the sofa.

She laughed as they both landed on it together. 'Hey, what's this for?'

His body was warm against hers. 'Just missed you,' he said.

He'd been at a hospital management meeting, and she knew that he hated those. It was part and parcel of being the head of the department, so there was no getting out of them.

'Want me to make you some food?' she murmured next to his ear.

He shook his head. 'Just coffee.' He lifted his head. 'Hannah still on her play date?'

She nodded. 'Hunter's mum phoned and asked if she could stay longer. It's an hour before we need to pick her up.'

Joshua let out a groan and rolled off her, changing position so he was sitting on the sofa. 'I don't think I'm cut out for this. What five-year-old girl goes on a play date with a boy? Shouldn't she be hanging out with other girls?'

Clara laughed. 'Stop being such an old guy. Hannah can go on play dates with whoever she likes. She's having fun, she's socialising; that's what's important.'

'Who is this Hunter anyhow?' asked Joshua. 'Do we know his mum and dad?'

She shook her head. 'Oh, no, we handed over our daughter to perfect strangers without a single question.'

The words were out before she'd even had a chance to think about them. But as soon as she said them out loud she froze.

Joshua's head whipped round and his gaze locked on her with such an intensity that her natural reaction was to back away. 'Slip of the tongue,' she said quickly as she stood up. 'I'll get the coffee.'

Her legs were shaking as she hurried into

the kitchen and she couldn't ignore the slight edge of panic in her chest.

She knew instinctively within a few seconds that Joshua was following her. She took a few quick deep breaths, trying to calm herself again. It was a genuine slip of the tongue. But it left her feeling exposed.

She stuck the pods into the coffee machine and kept breathing. Maybe this was a sign. Maybe it was time to have that conversation about Hannah that she'd been delaying.

As Joshua came around the corner into the kitchen, Clara spun around and put her hands behind her, leaning against the counter.

'We need to talk.' Their voices sounded in unison.

'Me first,' said Clara quickly.

'Okay.' Joshua nodded, his expression more serious than she'd ever seen before. It felt like being a child called into the headmaster's office. Which was ridiculous. Of course it was. But she couldn't pretend that wasn't how she felt.

'I need to talk to you about Hannah,' she said quickly.

'Okay.' His brow furrowed a little as if he wasn't quite sure where she was going with this.

And she wasn't. Instantly she wanted to

delay again because she was sure, no matter how she tried to frame this, Joshua would feel hurt. And it was the last thing she wanted to do. But she had to be truthful. She had to put Hannah first. Before her own wants and needs. And before Joshua's.

'Hannah spoke to me a few weeks ago about something. And I know I should have told you sooner but, to be honest, I've found it difficult to bring this up without hurting your feelings. Because that's not my intention, not at all.'

Joshua just looked confused. 'What do you mean?'

She sucked in a breath, willing herself to ignore the tears that materialised in her eyes. 'She was worried, Josh. I think she feels pressure—even though I know it's completely unintentional.'

'Pressure about what?' She could see he was starting to get a little annoyed.

'About her mum. About Abby.'

Joshua took a few steps closer. 'I don't understand.' The coffee machine started to make gurgling sounds behind her.

Clara closed her eyes for a second. 'It was bedtime and she was tired. She was talking. She told me she doesn't remember her mummy at all. And she's sad about it.'

Joshua shook his head. 'But she was just a baby—'

Clara put her hand up. 'I know that, and I explained to her that you and Georgie know that too. But she's sad. She's sad she can't remember anything—'

He cut her off. 'But that's why Georgie and I have told her as many stories as we can. So she knows it's okay to talk about her mum, to ask questions.'

Clara paused for a second, letting some silence fill that air between them. 'She feels guilty, Joshua. She feels guilty she can't remember, and she feels pressure to find memories that just aren't there.'

As Joshua's eyes widened, Clara added, 'She thinks it makes you sad.'

He took a step back, leaning against the wall in the kitchen. 'But—'

Nothing followed the word but she could see him trying to process what she'd just told him. His eyes fell on a pile of papers and cartons on the counter top that she'd been ready to take to recycling.

His voice trembled a little as he looked across at her. 'How long ago did she tell you this?'

Clara hesitated, inwardly cringing. 'A few weeks ago.'

'A few weeks ago, and you've said nothing?' There was no mistaking the incredulous tone in his voice.

Guilt flooded over her. 'I know. But I wasn't sure how to tell you. I've thought long and hard about it.'

'Did you think long and hard about how many times I might have mentioned Abby to Hannah over the last few weeks? How I might be unintentionally hurting my daughter without realising it?'

The wounded expression on his face told her everything she needed to know.

'I'm sorry,' she said quickly. 'But I did try and explain to her you didn't mean it. And I told her that maybe when she was older she might want to ask questions, and that you and Georgie would be happy to answer them.'

'You told my daughter all that, but you didn't think to sit me down and tell me too? To let me know that I'm clearly failing my daughter.' The words were spat out, and she knew he was angry, she knew he was hurt. Those words took her back to the first time he'd sat down on her sofa and opened up. Opened up about wondering if he was getting things right with Hannah. It was clear that those underlying fears had never left him.

She stepped forward but something in his

expression made her halt. 'You're a great dad, Joshua. Don't doubt it. Hannah is a lucky girl. And she's a real credit to you.'

Even as she said the words she could feel the shift in the air between them. It didn't matter that she was taking steps closer to him, it felt as though they were pulling further and further apart.

He shook his head and rested his hand on the countertop, not meeting her gaze. 'I can't believe you didn't talk to me about this right away. Don't you get how important this is?'

The implication in the words stung. She kept her voice low. 'I know how important it is. Why do you think we're having this conversation now? Do you think I wanted to do this? Do you really think I want to tell you not to talk about Abby to Hannah?' She held up her hands, 'How dare I? I didn't know Abby. I have no right to say something like that. Because I understand how hurtful it is.' She shook her head and looked down. 'I'm new to all this parenting stuff, Joshua. You know that. But I know what the right thing is. And this,' she pointed her finger down to the floor and said the words a little more resolutely, 'is the right thing to do. Because you and I aren't the important ones here. Hannah is.'

'You think you need to tell me that?' His voice was raised, cutting through the kitchen.

Clara threw her hands back up. 'Of course I don't. But you're so angry at me right now I think you need a reminder.'

Joshua turned his back on her, leaning over the counter top, his eyes fixed downwards. Clara wasn't sure what to say next. She was trying to quell the tightness in her chest. A few days ago, everything had been perfect between them. Should she have kept quiet—said nothing at all? But what kind of person actually did that—didn't loving someone mean loving all of them, and not being afraid to talk about the hard stuff?

She turned and pulled out the cups from beneath the machine. She wasn't even thirsty, and if she could pick a drink right now it wouldn't be coffee. But it gave her something to do with her hands. Something for her brain to focus on while Joshua's brain focused on how much he hated her, and what a bad parent he was.

But the next words she heard were totally unexpected. 'Clara, what are these?'

She turned back around. He had an empty cardboard pill box in one hand and a catalogue in the other. The sperm donor catalogue. The things she'd planned on placing in the recycling bin.

Her heart stopped.

Joshua was shaking his head and looking thoroughly confused. 'Are you trying to have a child?' he asked.

The words stuck somewhere in her throat. This wasn't a conversation she'd ever planned to have with him. 'I… I…considered it,' she said finally.

'You considered it?' he repeated, disbelief on his face.

She nodded and swallowed. Coffee might be useful right now. Her mouth had never been so dry.

'And this is another thing you didn't think to mention?'

She shifted uncomfortably, but somewhere deep inside she felt a little flicker of anger. 'I didn't mention it because it didn't affect you. This was something I was considering before I came down here. I hadn't decided if it was a step I wanted to take, but I wanted to find out more, so I did.'

'And you didn't think it important enough to mention to me—even though we were in a relationship?'

When he said those words out loud, it made

her feel ridiculous. Even though it all made perfect sense in her head.

Something flickered across his gaze. 'And was IVF with a sperm donor the only way you considered having a baby?' Ice dripped from his words so clearly it made her shiver as the implication penetrated her brain.

'What?' She couldn't help but raise her voice. Surely he couldn't be accusing her of *that*?

He kept his gaze locked firmly on hers. 'Answer the question.'

She couldn't believe it. She couldn't believe his brain would actually work that way. 'You'd better be joking,' she snapped, her temper finally fraying.

Joshua started pacing. 'Why would I be joking, Clara? The person that I've told that I love, that I want to make plans with, has been keeping secrets from me. I thought I knew you—but it turns out I don't know you at all. Maybe this relationship is all just a convenience to you. Charm the local guy and see if you can get pregnant. Is that what I was to you—a convenience?'

Now she was shouting and she couldn't stop herself. She didn't allow herself to start where he had just left off. She started with the whole ridiculous idea. 'Are you crazy? What I feel about you is hardly convenient. How could it be? In a few weeks we'll be parted again. You'll be here and I'll be back in Edinburgh. The job swap will be over. I won't get to see you every day. I won't get to run up the stairs and knock on your door whenever I need a Josh fix. I won't get to pretend to want to use the gym just to see you in those shorts. What part of being hundreds of miles apart seems convenient to you?' She took another breath. 'And then, on top of all that, you make stupid claims. That I'm using you as a potential sperm donor. Words can't even describe how insulted I am. You honestly think I would do something like that? Casually sleep around and try to get pregnant. Just what kind of human being do you think I am?' Angry tears started to spill down her cheeks. She needed to get her temper in check. Her brain wanted to transport her body to the gym upstairs so she could have a go at one of the punch bags. It might be the only way to let all this pent-up frustration out.

Joshua was still shaking his head. He picked up the cardboard pill box. This time his voice was quiet. This time his voice sounded sad. 'And why didn't you tell me about these?'

She blinked, becoming automatically defensive. After a few moments of deep breathing she tilted her chin upwards. 'Because what prescription medication I take is my business. I don't need to share that with you. You've been in this job a long time, Joshua. I know lots of doctors who've taken anti-depressants, now, and in the past. It's a stressful job. Things happen. And sometimes you need to seek treatment. I'm not ashamed. I'm not embarrassed. This has been part of my life for a long time, and I've accepted it. I also don't think I need to explain myself to you. I'd actually just decided that I was feeling well enough to come off my meds, but again, that's nothing to do with you.'

He turned back to the counter and pressed his hands against it, bowing his head. By the time he turned back around she was stunned to see he had tears in his eyes.

'I can't do this,' he said simply.

'What?'

'I've lived this life. It almost broke me. I can't do it again.'

'What are you talking about?'

'I had a wife who kept secrets from me. She knew she was sick. She knew the treatment could harm our baby. She chose not to share with me. She chose to keep it to herself until after she'd delivered our baby.' He paused and she could see the hurt on his face and in his eyes. 'She didn't trust me enough to tell me.'

The words sliced through her. More than she expected them to.

He shook his head again and, although there was a tremble to his voice, it also seemed firm. 'I can't be with someone like that again. Someone who can't trust me with their personal issues. Someone who keeps secrets.'

She knew he wasn't talking about the sperm donor. She knew he was talking about her mental health.

Part of her felt guilty. She'd never thought about this from his perspective before. She'd been so worried about hurting his feelings over the conversation about Hannah that she hadn't even considered this—even though she knew his history. Why hadn't she made the connection? It made her feel stupid.

'Talking about mental health isn't easy.' She started slowly, meeting his gaze again. 'Particularly when the person you're going to talk to is also technically your boss.' His expression remained unmoved.

'If I tell people I suffer from depression then—no matter who they are—a judgement forms in their brain. *She can't cope. She isn't grateful for what she's got. She can't be relied on. Don't give her more than one thing to do. What on earth has she got to be depressed about?* I've heard them all, Joshua. So I stopped talking about it.' She held up one hand. 'How do you explain depression when you can't link it to one thing? How do you explain that you just lose interest in things you previously loved? That you can't find the energy to get out of your chair, let alone do an extra shift? That the edges around your world feel dull and greyish? The first thing people ask is why? What they can do to help. What they can do to make you better.' She sucked in a deep breath as her voice started to shake. 'I guess somehow I thought that you might be like that, Joshua. That you might try to—' she lifted her fingers '—fix me.'

Another tear rolled down her cheek. 'I don't want you to fix me. I don't want anyone to fix me.' She pressed a hand to her chest. 'Because this is me. This is who I am. And I want to fix myself. And you have to take me as I am, Joshua. All of me. Even the parts you don't like.'

He blinked, clearly slightly stunned by her words. One minute both had been raising their voices, now they were speaking in barely a whisper, so much hurt in the air between them.

Clara blinked, trying to pull back the memories of their weekend together and how they'd been so happy. Life had seemed almost perfect. She'd met a man she loved, with a little girl she adored. Work was great, and they were making plans for a future together. Maybe that future could include the large family she'd always wanted?

Now, because of one conversation, everything had become unpicked. Had they ever really known each other at all?

The realisation made her sway and she clutched the counter behind her.

Joshua squeezed his eyes closed for a second. She could almost hear his brain ticking—and she couldn't even begin to guess what he might be thinking.

His voice remained low. 'I thought we were good together. I thought we loved each other and could find a way to make this work. I thought I might have found someone who would love my daughter just as much as I do.'

Those words made the tears start to stream again.

'But I can't risk my heart, or hers, with someone who doesn't trust me. I would never have judged you. I would never have tried to fix you. I wanted to love all of you, not just the parts you let me see.' He gave a hollow laugh. 'I didn't think you were perfect, Clara, but I thought you were perfect for me.' He lowered his head one final time. 'Seems like I was wrong.'

And then he turned and walked out of the door.

For a moment she was stunned. Her first reaction was to run after him. But too much had been said. She still felt as if she couldn't process most of it.

Her heart started fluttering rapidly in her chest and she couldn't quite get a breath. Her legs crumpled under her in the kitchen and her body moved into self-protect mode.

She moved her head between her legs, ignoring the heartbeat she could now feel pulsing in her ears and counted to ten, trying to slow down her breathing.

Her brain felt foggy and muddled. Her first instinct was to look at her watch, but she avoided it, not wanting to become more panicked. She willed her heart to slow. She knew exactly what was happening to her. She'd seen it happen to other people—she'd even treated other people having panic attacks—she'd just never expected to have one herself.

She stayed where she was for the longest time, waiting until her breathing and heart rate eventually slowed. Eventually, with shaking legs, she stood.

She grabbed a glass and filled it with water,

taking a few sips before setting it back on the counter. Alongside the untouched coffee cups.

It was as if someone had reached inside her chest and given her heart a sharp twist.

Those two cups. When she'd started the process she'd just had that slip of the tongue about 'our' daughter. Because in a few short months that was how she felt about Hannah. Joshua and Hannah were her family. The people she should be with. The place her heart told her she belonged.

She moved out of the kitchen and through to her bedroom, sagging down on her bed.

Except...it wasn't her bed. It would never be her bed. It was Georgie's.

The view from the window would never be hers. Her view was one of fields and sheep. One of emptiness, bleakness and loneliness.

Her cottage had never conjured feelings like these before. The comfort she usually felt from memories of her own place was gone. Now, it just seemed like a space for someone who'd made mistakes. Who'd lost the people she loved.

And would probably never feel whole again.

CHAPTER TWELVE

JOSHUA DRIFTED FROM one day to the next. It was amazing how easy it was to purposely avoid someone at work. Every time he caught a glimpse of her slim frame or white coat he would find something else to focus on entirely. Whether that was giving the conversation he was having with someone else his full attention or concentrating completely on tests results or case notes, he found he could easily keep his eyes glued on one subject.

It was his other senses that objected. They seemed to scream from every pore of his body. He would catch her scent from across the room or around a corner. He would hear her voice or laughter in conversation with other members of staff. His stomach clenched when he saw a wrapper from her favourite chocolate bar in one of the bins under the desk on the ward. As for his skin? It seemed to permanently tingle. An ache had formed underneath his fingertips. Letting him know they were missing something, mimicking the ache in his heart.

He caught sight of a few curious glances. The other staff obviously knew something was amiss. But no one had dared ask him.

He could hardly blame them. He snapped when anyone second-guessed an order that he gave, changed off duty rotas with little consultation to avoid being on shift with Clara, and didn't have his usual patience for the job.

All the time he was constantly aware of the days ticking past in his head, like some enormous game show timer. She'd be gone in a matter of weeks. And even though his head told him he should be relieved, his heart ached so badly he wondered if he'd ever stop thinking he might actually have chest pain.

His pager sounded late one night and he picked it up and sighed. The call took minutes. He'd have to go in. But he had no one to look after Hannah. On previous occasions he would have picked up the phone to Clara. Before Clara, he'd had his sister or his nanny, but now his options were limited.

He bundled Hannah up in blankets and carried her out to the car. It was less than ideal.

By the time he reached the ward, the doctor who'd called him had started to panic. He was surprised to find Ron at the desk—he normally worked day hours.

Ron held out his arms for Hannah as Joshua strode into the ward. 'My fault, sorry,' he said. 'It's my niece and Reuben seemed out of his depth.'

Joshua nodded. Reuben, the doctor on duty, *had* been out of his depth—he'd known that from the call. Joshua could see what must be Ron's sister and husband crowded around the bed of a small, pale child, wired up to a monitor that showed her heart rate was way too fast.

Joshua took a breath and put his hand on Ron's arm. 'Don't worry,' he said reassuringly. 'I'll look after your niece.'

And he did. The little girl had a high temperature due to chickenpox. The spots came out gradually over the next few hours. But the temperature led to the discovery of an undiagnosed heart murmur, causing lots of extra beats and a worrying ECG. Joshua called in a cardiac colleague who, in turn, discovered an issue with the little girl's heart valve. Treatment was started promptly, and as soon as her temperature started to come down her heart rate came back to normal limits.

It was four hours before Joshua had a chance to sit back down at the desk with a partly relieved Ron. 'Where's Hannah?'

'In a makeshift bed I made for her in the duty room. Clara's with her.'

'What?' It was the last thing Joshua expected to hear.

Ron sighed and shook his head. 'She woke up and, even though she knows me, she was scared. You were busy looking after my niece, so I called Clara. She was here within ten minutes and is curled up with Hannah now.' He ran a hand through his hair. 'Why didn't you leave Hannah with her?'

Joshua was trying to ignore the prickle of anger that he felt. Ron had prioritised. He knew that Joshua needed to focus on his niece. So he'd left him to focus on his job, while sorting out things for Hannah. He knew it was reasonable.

He took his time before he spoke. 'Clara and I aren't together any more. It wouldn't be fair for me to ask her to watch Hannah.' He paused, then added, 'I wish you'd asked me before you called her.'

Ron gave him a hard stare and lowered his head closer to Joshua's. It was still the middle of the night and most of the ward was in darkness.

'Josh, you're my colleague and I respect you. When Kelly was sick tonight, you were the one person I wanted to see her. When I knew that Reuben was panicking, I insisted he call you. For kids, you're the best there is. But for life? You're a halfwit.'

Joshua was stunned. In all the years they'd worked together, Ron had been always been straight talking, but never quite *this* blunt. Ron pushed his chair back. 'I'm not going to give you a lecture because I've no right to. But everyone has spent the last week tiptoeing around you. This place is too busy for nonsense like that. I asked your daughter who she wanted when she was upset. She said one name. Clara. That's why I phoned her.'

He pointed to the duty room. 'You look terrible and so does Clara. Everyone can see it. Whatever is wrong, it's time to sort it out—for all our sakes.' He put a hand on Joshua's shoulder. 'So, for tonight, and for what happens in the future with Kelly, thank you, Joshua. Thank you for coming in and looking after my niece. I trust you. I trust your judgement.' He gave a sad smile as he looked at the door of the duty room. 'But do you trust your own?'

Clara had been surprised when the phone had woken her in the middle of the night. Most doctors had internal radar. The nights they were supposed to be on call, they never truly slept properly, always waiting for a pager to sound, or a phone to ring. But on the nights they weren't on call most slept like the dead.

It only took a few moments to grasp the situation and, even in her befuddled state, she was already out of bed and opening her wardrobe before the conversation was over.

As she'd arrived she hadn't even looked along the corridor to where she guessed Joshua was. She'd gone straight to the duty room where Ron sat with a sniffing Hannah and gathered her up into her arms, letting her snuggle in to get the sleep she so badly needed.

She'd taken Ron's hand. 'I hope your niece is okay. I'm sure Joshua will get her sorted.'

Ron gave her a worried smile. 'I hope so,' he said before disappearing out of the door.

Clara sat for a while, thoughts spinning around her head. This had become the normal for her. Going over and over what she could have done differently. How things might have gone if Joshua hadn't looked at the pile of recycling at the end of the counter.

It was odd. But somehow it felt as if it was meant to happen. At first she'd been angry and annoyed at his reaction to both things: the potential look for a sperm donor, and the empty packet of tablets.

But time and clarity had made her realise how damaging keeping secrets had been for him. The truth was, telling Joshua earlier would never have changed his wife's outcome. But maybe it would have changed how he lived with himself after.

The door opened, letting in a sliver of light from the ward. She raised her head as Joshua took a few steps into the room and closed the door behind him.

There was silence for a few seconds. Just his presence made her skin prickle and as the familiar smell from his quickly sprayed deodorant drifted across the room towards her she blinked away the damp feeling in her eyes. 'Ron's niece is going to be okay,' he said in a gravelly tone. 'She'll need surgery at some point, to sort her valve. But everything is manageable.'

Clara gave a sigh of relief for Ron, the quiet backbone of the paediatric unit. His family lived on the opposite side of London, but when there had been trouble he'd brought his niece here, to the people he trusted to look after his family. To Joshua.

There were only a few weeks left. Soon she'd be gone from all this. And the startling realisation for her was, no matter how bad things were, she didn't want to be away from this. She didn't want to be away from him, or Hannah. Not ever.

He took a seat opposite her. 'Thank you,' he said in a low voice.

'You should have called me,' she answered quickly.

He sighed. 'I didn't like to. I didn't think I could. Not the way things are between us.'

'We're adults,' she said as a tear spilled down her cheek. 'We can fight all we want. It doesn't need to affect Hannah. We have to do better than this.'

She could sense him holding his breath. The warmth from Hannah's little body against hers was flooding through her. This was the life she wanted. With this prickly, sometimes argumentative man.

'I don't want you to go,' he said so softly she thought she'd imagined it.

'What?'

He raised his head and looked at her across the dark room. She could only see him because the blind on the window wasn't down. 'I don't want you to go,' he repeated thickly. 'No matter what's happened, how I felt about things—I don't want you to go. I love you, Clara. Things are tough, but I've learned enough in this life to know that if you find love, only a fool lets it slip through their fingers.'

She couldn't speak, her words sticking in her throat.

'I want this to work. But I need honesty. I need us to be an open book to each other. I don't want to fix you, Clara. I just want to understand how you're feeling. If you're struggling, tell me. If you're not, tell me. I just need to know there are no secrets between us. I have to be able to trust you.'

She blinked back the tears in her eyes. 'I don't want to leave either,' she breathed. 'I was wondering how to tell your sister that I don't want to go back to my job in Edinburgh. To ask if she'd consider staying.' She let out a quiet laugh. 'I was looking at jobs in London last night. Wondering where I could find some place down here. I'm sorry, Joshua, I've had some time to think about it from your perspective. The truth is, I'm not used to sharing. I've spent so long keeping things inside. There's still such a stigma around depression—even though we both know lots of our colleagues suffer. I wasn't sure how you would react, or what you would say.' She glanced down at Hannah as her voice broke. 'You might have questioned my ability to do my job. Or you might have thought I wasn't good enough for you and Hannah.'

He was in front of her in an instant, his hands cupping her face. 'No. Don't say that. Not ever. I would never think like that. I love you, Clara, and everything that comes with you. I overreacted before. All I could think about was how hurt I'd been. How I hated the thought of someone I loved keeping secrets from me.' He pulled one hand down and put it on his heart. 'I know I can't live like that. I hadn't realised how damaged I'd been before. How much losing Abby had affected my ability to form other relationships. Before, I always had excuses. I didn't want to get close to someone. I didn't want to find out they'd kept something from me, or lied to me about something, because I wasn't sure I could survive that again. It was easier just to keep myself in a box. To not expose myself to the possibilities.' He took a deep breath. 'You were the first person who made me want to put my heart on the line again. You, Clara.'

She blinked as tears streamed down her face. Her words faltered. 'You were the only person I've ever thought could give me the life I wanted. The happiness. The family I always dreamed of. I just didn't know how to tell you. To share with you.'

His fingers brushed a tear from her cheek. 'I love you. Please tell me that we can both learn how to share. I don't expect perfect—because I know I'm far from perfect. But I've found someone who makes me want to live life again. Who loves my daughter just as dearly as she loves me.' He took a breath. 'And who wasn't afraid to put Hannah before me, before us.' He looked into her eyes. 'I understand that now. I understand how hard that must have been. And I know it was completely and utterly the right thing to do. I'll get better at all this, Clara, I promise.'

Clara took a few shuddering breaths. 'So, you can accept me as I am? Knowing that sometimes I might feel unwell. And you can't fix me. You can love that part of me, just as much as the rest of me?'

He nodded. 'Of course, Clara. It's you. It's part of you. Whatever you need, I'm here.'

She nodded slowly, letting the warm feeling inside her spread. Acceptance. Acceptance for now, and for always. No need to lie about how she was feeling. No need to paint a smile on her face and pretend things were always fine. The feeling of relief was overwhelming. 'And what about later?'

'Later?'

'When I ask you about my other dreams.'

His brow furrowed slightly. 'What other dreams?'

'Dreams about having a big family. Could you see that being part of our future?'

His face broke into a smile. 'If we're blessed

with a family, I'll be delighted. If that doesn't happen, we can look at other plans. As long as we do it together, I'm happy.' He clasped both her hands. 'Just promise me you'll stay. You make our lives complete. We don't want to do this without you.'

The tears were well and truly flowing now. She pulled him towards her, so his mouth was only inches from hers, with only Hannah's small body between them. 'I'm only going to say yes if you kiss me and promise to keep kissing me, now and for ever,' breathed Clara, her heart racing in her chest.

His lips brushed ever so gently against hers. 'I can make the promise…' his fingers tangled in her hair as his lips met hers again '…now and for ever.'

EPILOGUE

THEY WERE IN LUCK. It was the one sunny day of the year in Scotland.

It was strange being back in her old house. It was even stranger sharing her old bedroom with Georgie as they both got dressed for their double wedding.

Their dresses were entirely different. Georgie's was more fairy tale with cream lace, slightly off the shoulder and three-quarter-length. She had tiny flowers woven through her hair, and her three-month-old baby lay kicking in the crib in the centre of the room.

Clara laughed as she held her breath and Georgie zipped her into her close-fitting, full-length gown. Outside, the white marquee flapped in the wind. They'd decided on a more informal wedding with a marquee in the field next door. Clara only hoped the farmer had managed to keep the sheep away. She stared down at her gown. 'How long before this is covered in mud?' she said, laughing.

Georgie fastened her short veil onto Clara's head. 'About five minutes, give or take how long it takes Truffle to jump up on you.'

She squeezed Clara's arm. 'I'm so happy that my brother met you.'

Clara held up one finger. 'Don't. You'll get us both crying again. I've never seen Ryan this happy. And as for baby Isla. You're making me broody.' They both turned to where Isla was lying happily kicking in her crib with a big smile on her face.

There was a noise at the door. 'Come on, girls. Let's get this show on the road.'

The door swung open and both fathers were waiting outside. Hannah was jumping up and down in her long pink dress. 'Hurry up!'

Georgie's mum came inside and picked up her tiny granddaughter. 'Daddy's waiting for you.' She smiled, before stopping to give each bride a kiss on the cheek.

'Ready?' Clara asked Georgie. They both nodded and made their way down the spiral staircase without tripping.

The wind caught their dresses as they walked towards the marquee, each on the arm of their father.

Clara's breath caught in her throat as she

saw Ryan and Joshua waiting next to an archway of flowers, both dressed in kilts. Ryan had Isla in his arms and was beaming as he waited for his bride. Joshua looked decidedly nervous, but as Hannah tore down the aisle in front of them he swept her up in his arms and shot Clara a grin. 'Gorgeous,' he mouthed to her.

Warmth flooded through her. All their family and friends were here. The double wedding had been her idea. As soon as she'd met Georgie she knew she was perfect for Ryan, and that she had another friend for life.

Three months ago, she and Joshua had sat nervously in the waiting room for news of their niece or nephew. By the time Ryan had emerged from the labour suite, his eyes bright with delight, and the words *'It's a girl!'* she'd known she'd never need to worry about her friend again.

Their friends laughed as Truffle came down the aisle with the rings attached to his collar. There was no way that Ryan wouldn't let him be part of the day.

She slid her hands into Joshua's as they said their vows. No matter the chaos around them, he only had eyes for her. The marquee fell silent as he recited the vows that he'd written.

'Clara, you breezed into my life when I least expected it and swept me away with your sass, your straight talk and sincerity. I didn't know what I was missing until I met you. You embraced both myself and Hannah and made us feel truly loved. I learned how to trust again. Know that I will love you now and for ever. You bring such joy into our lives. On good days and bad I will love you. In joy and sadness I will love you. In old age and wrinkles I will love you.'

The congregation let out a laugh before he continued.

He reached up and touched her cheek. 'Whatever life throws at us, Hannah and I will love you, because we can do anything with you at our side.'

There was a collective sigh around the room and then Clara said her own vows back.

'When I first met you I called you Mr Grumpy. I didn't realise what a big heart was hiding inside that chest of yours. Thank you for loving me and accepting me the way I am. Thank you for trusting me with your heart and with your daughter's. I promise to always take care of them, and any other children that might come along. Thank you for bringing joy into my life and a sense of belonging, a new family, and for letting me experience the joy of parenting a wonderful little girl with you. Thank you for letting me realise that being together takes

254 FAMILY FOR THE CHILDREN'S DOC

work, commitment and the biggest amount of love in the world. I'll love you always.'

Joshua let Hannah take their rings from Truffle and pass them over to them, sliding hers onto her finger.

Ryan took a little longer, getting tearful through his vows, before juggling baby Isla and finally managing to slide the wedding ring onto Georgie's finger.

'Finally!' Georgie said gleefully when the celebrant announced they could finally kiss.

Joshua slid his hands around Clara's waist and held her tightly. 'I agree,' he whispered. 'Finally.' His lips met hers and he dipped her backwards as she slid her hands around his neck.

And Clara knew that life was perfect.

* * * * *